KT-362-802

SHELLEY SMITH

---◆---

THE MISSING SCHOOLGIRL

& OTHER STORIES

Complete and Unabridged

LIBRARIES NI
WITHDRAWN FROM STOCK

LINFORD
Leicester

First published in Great Britain

First Linford Edition
published 2018

Copyright © 1945, 1955, 1957, 1969,
1970, 1971 by Shelley Smith
Copyright © 2017 by the Estate of Shelley Smith
All rights reserved

A catalogue record for this book is available
from the British Library.

ISBN 978–1–4448–3700–1

Published by
F. A. Thorpe (Publishing)
Anstey, Leicestershire

Set by Words & Graphics Ltd.
Anstey, Leicestershire
Printed and bound in Great Britain by
T. J. International Ltd., Padstow, Cornwall

This book is printed on acid-free paper

Contents

The Missing Schoolgirl

The room waited, listening to the silence. Imperceptibly, shadows gathered in the corners. Once, the woman raised her head from her sewing to glance towards the window where an orange cloud trailed its expansive glory, and bent again over her work. The brass desk handles winked at the crystal vase in the firelight.

It was quiet. So quiet that all the minute sounds which make up the orchestra of silence could be distinctly heard (the delicate pizzicato of her needle clicking against the darner as it wove in and out, the muted cello of the woollen thread drawn through the stuff . . . the fluttering woodwind of flames and the coals' tinselly crackle . . . the occasional fluting bubble of the man's pipe, a page turning, and the drumbeat of his shoe knocking against the fender as he shifted his feet).

He leaned forward, his eyes still on his

book, and with a brisk gesture sent a stream of moisture from his pipe-stem hissing into the fire. 'Sorry, dear,' he murmured, some faint string of recollection tugging his absent mind.

The Merrimans were ordinary people, contented with their uneventful lives, fretted by no more than the common anxieties of existence — worries over the children's health, bills: no monstrous tragedy had ever loomed at them from beyond the safe confines of their small neat lives.

Merriman ran the local estate agency. He was a lean, gentle creature with a tired parchment face. He worked hard and was devoted to his wife (in twelve years he had never looked at another woman) and proud of their children. An ordinary family.

The room, curiously colourless and impersonal, as if all the life had been tidied out of it, did in fact reveal Mrs. Merriman's nature. She was a woman possessed by a driving passion: the need to impose order and an impeccable cleanliness on her surroundings — as though the darkness and chaos lurking beneath the surface of life could thus be kept at bay. All was so bright, one had the impression that even the flames in the small fire had been polished, and the sole ornament, a brass ashtray that stood above the tiled surround, glittered like winter sunlight.

Mrs. Merriman was a slender, neat woman, very quiet, with an odd trick of keeping her large, full-lidded eyes from meeting another's gaze.

Every time the wind sent the branch of the lilac tree tapping against the wall outside she looked up, mistaking it for a light footstep. The orange cloud had drifted away, leaving behind some fragments of dark worsted on a sky of Chinese yellow. From where she sat she could see the flowering cherry in the road, its coarse pink blossoms transmuted to tender mauve in the fading light.

A vague awareness of his wife's restless glances window-wards caused Mr. Merriman, a finger marking his place, to look up and ask if he should draw the curtains.

'Not just yet, dear,' Mrs. Merriman

murmured, apparently preoccupied in snipping her thread and patting the darned place smooth.

He doubted that she could see, but he read on a few moments longer till the print sank into the twilit page; then he rose and switched on the light.

Instinctively her head turned again to the window, which in that instant had become a deep transparent blue, like an immense sapphire. Her husband settled back in his chair and plunged his mind once more into the torrid landscape. Without conscious thought the woman folded and unfolded a pair of socks, running her hand inside them, stretching them against her fingers to find the thin places, and rolling them up again.

The polished crimson petals of a tulip leaning from the crystal vase parted suddenly from its indigo heart and plopped with an effect of startling loudness onto the table. As if released from a spell, as if this was the excuse she had been waiting for, she rose and tidily collected the fallen petals, crushing their coolness for an instant in her fingers before she dropped them into the wastepaper basket, and then moved across to the window, cupping her hands against the dark pane. There was nothing to be seen but the dusky restless movement of the ornamental cherry on the pavement. Its pretty gaiety had vanished with the daylight and it stirred now with a mysterious life of its own that was oddly sinister. As she stood there, pressing her cheek to the cold glass, a distant street light sprang up, sending its long pale beams shivering through the leaves. Now it was night.

Mrs. Merriman's incapacity was in uttering her thoughts aloud. A formidable shyness clamped down on her tongue, locking it as it locked her gaze. She dreaded exposing herself to the least human contact. It was hard for her to express the simplest thought. With her husband this didn't matter, because people who have lived long together can perfectly understand each other without words. So now Mr. Merriman, lost as he was among jacaranda trees and burning sunlight, yet in a secondary consciousness

— the physical consciousness that was aware of the warmth of the fire on his legs — was fidgeted by his wife's unease.

'What's the matter, dear?' he mumbled, as if he was talking in his sleep.

'Nell's late,' she just audibly said.

Her husband uttered a sound intended to convey attention, understanding and sympathy.

Mrs. Merriman stroked the folded curtain, its softness offering a comforting sensation to her mind, and elaborated.

'I did say she was to be home before dark. She knows she has her prep still to do.'

'It's not really late,' he answered from far away.

She gave a faint sigh. Not late, but *dark* — darkness was worse. It was perhaps this that rendered her uneasy. She could not speak of the little premonition of fear that haunted her mind. In the silence the fire shifted and sank together. She knelt before the grate, carefully tonging pieces of coal onto the crimson glow.

Merriman's eye wavered from his book.

'She'll be back soon,' he said.

She made no answer, tidying the hearth.

A thought came between him and the page, and he looked up to say with more attentiveness, 'You do know where she is, I suppose?'

'She's gone to tea with Sally.'

'Well, then,' he said easily. 'You know how it is. They forget the time when they're enjoying themselves, poor little blighters.'

Her husband's attitude was so much more reasonable, so much more natural than her own that she was ashamed not to be quite assured by it. And yet . . . the point was . . . She brought herself with an effort to explain the point:

'It's just that I don't like her to be out alone after dark.'

'She's not a baby, she's a big girl; she can take care of herself,' he averred.

She gazed into the heart of the fire, her face dusted with reddish light and mournful shadows. He watched her; a smile touched the corners of his mouth.

'Want me to go and fetch her?' he said generously, clapping shut his book.

For a mere instant her great eyes glanced into his. 'It's a shame to trouble you,' she murmured.

'No trouble, madam; it's all part of the Merriman service,' he said, getting up with a yawn and stretching. 'A breath of air'll do me good,' he added, bending to shake up his cushion with a gesture that after twelve years' training had become automatic. 'Be back in a jiffy.' He stretched again and ruffled his fine hair. 'Think I won't take the car; I might miss her if she's already started.'

The evening was pleasantly mild, stars glinting between pale clouds. The Cathcarts, Sally's parents, lived barely ten minutes away. Even at that early hour the streets were almost empty. He strolled along, enjoying his agreeable solitariness, amusing himself with the idea of the various scenes in the human comedy playing out behind the discreetly curtained windows, a luminous amber or crimson on the darkness. Once at an intersection a small figure approached and he hurried towards it, but passing beneath a street lamp it became a schoolboy in a blue cap.

As the long rectangle of light from the Cathcarts' doorway fell across him, Merriman said cheerily: 'I've come to collect my young scamp.'

Cathcart, laconic, in his shabby polo sweater, a spanner dangling from his free hand, surveyed him.

'I don't think we've got her, have we?' he said vaguely. He tossed the spanner and caught it. 'Come inside. I'll ask the wife.' He put his foot on the bottom stair and called: 'Julia!'

There was a rush of footsteps overhead and a woman's voice hissed from the banisters:

'Freddy, for goodness' sake! *Must* you — '

'Merriman's here,' he interjected.

'I'm afraid I've come at an awkward time,' Merriman began as she ran downstairs to greet him, smoothing her dress.

'Not a bit,' she cried in her rusty, alluring voice. 'Come in, come in. What's the matter with Fred? Why on earth didn't he take you into the sitting-room? I

11

must apologize for my husband, the man's dotty,' she said, giving him a wide, glittering smile.

'No, really!' He took a step backwards. 'I've only looked in to pick up Nell.'

Her eyes widened.

'Nell? But Nell's not here,' she said.

'Oh!' He looked puzzled. 'Then somehow I must have missed her. When did she leave?'

She gave him a strange, thoughtful look.

'Leave here, do you mean?' Her husky voice carefully empty of expression, she said: 'You must have got it wrong. We haven't seen her today.'

He began to speak, and paused, feeling a fool.

'Must have got it wrong, then,' he agreed. 'But I thought Jackie said . . . ' His words died away. It was no good arguing about it, but Jackie certainly had said 'with Sally'.

'Lost your little girl?' said Cathcart, drifting back with his spanner.

'We must try and *think* where else she might be,' Julia Cathcart declared, slaying her husband with her eyes while she shed over Merriman a brilliant unconvincing smile.

A door at the back of the hall burst open and a huge child shot out, her tongue falling out of her mouth in an idiot's grimace when she saw them there blocking her way.

'Oh, Sally! Come here a minute,' said her mother. 'She may know where Nell is,' she explained, turning to the man beside her.

The only possible method of advancing on a group of adults when they happen to be watching you is to leap for the banister rail, swing one's feet between the rises, and nonchalantly descend that way, one's behind swaying in the air like a barrage balloon.

'Don't you say good evening to Mr. Merriman?' her mother inquired in a level tone.

'Hullo,' the child said, hanging head down by her knees from the rail to account for the flood of scarlet in her face.

'Could you,' said Mrs. Cathcart harshly,

13

'for just two minutes try to remember that you're a human being and not an ape?'

The child giggled sheepishly and leaped from the stairs, landing on her father's foot.

'Steady, Mrs. Hippo,' he said, tapping her skull lightly with the spanner.

'Sally, did Nell tell you where she was going this afternoon?'

'No,' she said casually, swinging on her father's arm. 'No one knew.'

Mrs. Cathcart frowned.

'What do you mean, no one knew? Do leave your father alone and pay attention.'

'No one knew why she wasn't at school. Miss Forrester asked us if anyone knew if she'd got ill or anything, because she seemed all right in the morning.'

'You mean, Nell didn't go to school this afternoon?'

The child assented, in a tone that clearly expressed her never-failing amazement at the stupidity of grown-ups: wasn't that what she'd been *saying*? Why did they have to keep asking the same thing over and over again?

There was an uncomfortable moment

while the eyes of the adults met in consternation and slid uneasily away. Then Mrs. Cathcart briskly told Sally to run along, and they watched in silence the child banging her way up the stairs.

'Aren't they devils,' Mrs. Cathcart said brightly with an insincere groan. 'One simply daren't guess what they'll be up to next. But I honestly wouldn't *worry*. Nell's a fearfully sensible child. She'll probably be home when you get back.'

'Yes,' Merriman agreed blankly. 'Yes. I . . . ' he murmured, and continued to stand there like a stock or stone, as if he had forgotten his whereabouts, as if he had no notion what to do next.

Cathcart, to put an end to it, said: 'Have a drink before you go.'

At which Merriman started, came to himself, and said quickly, 'Better get on. Thanks all the same.'

There were other schoolfriends she might be with, he told himself as he walked sharply down the road, the only sound his footsteps ringing on the pavement. For half an hour or more he wandered about the district, knocking up people he scarcely knew to inquire idiotically: 'I wonder if my little girl is with you, by any chance?'

The small hope he was nourishing that Nell might be back died as soon as he saw his wife's face. Supper was a wretched affair. Mrs. Merriman sat at the table, not even pretending to eat, shielding her eyes with her hand.

'I'm so afraid,' she muttered, pushing aside her untouched plate. 'Such terrible things happen nowadays.' Even to utter the words 'Look at all the children who are run over every day' was so unbearable that she rose brusquely and went to the window, drawing aside the curtain to stare into the night, streaked to her tear-filled eyes with the trembling shimmer of the street-lamp's beams.

'Look, dear,' he said, 'if she was knocked down, it must have been locally and we should have heard by now.' He had not dared to tell her the child had not been to school that afternoon. He folded his napkin methodically and stood up.

'I'm going out again,' he said abruptly. 'We can't go on sitting here, waiting and fretting our hearts out, it's too stupid. I shall try the cinemas. I've an idea she may have gone to the pictures — isn't that what children mostly do when they play truant? She's probably thoroughly enjoying herself watching the programme round over and over again, without a thought for her poor silly parents,' he said with assumed cheerfulness.

Merriman had the impression on his subsequent return that his wife had actually not moved since he left her; the clotted plates were still on the table where they had been untidily pushed aside. He braced himself against the weariness that seemed to weigh on his shoulders like a heavy cloak.

'You didn't find her,' she said, tears springing to her eyes.

'No, I didn't find her.' He ran his tongue over his dry lips and said quickly, 'At all events, she's not been injured. I phoned the hospital.' He saw his wife's face lighten in a flash of relief, and then darken again with a new anxiety.

'Oh, God, where can she be?' he heard her whisper. 'She's never done anything like this before. I know something terrible has happened. I can *feel* it.' Her thin, large-knuckled hands knotted painfully together.

'Now, dear,' he said. 'Now, dear.'

But she tore herself from his grasp.

'Clive, I'm going to look for her. I can't stand it any more . . . this *waiting* . . . this terrible *waiting* . . . '

'I know, dear, I know. But don't go just yet. Someone is coming and you'll need to be here.' He paused. 'Jackie, I went to the police station; they're sending round a sergeant.'

Perhaps it was better for her to cry, he thought, stroking her hair, murmuring sounds of comfort.

She did not know herself whether she was crying with relief that something was to be done at last, or shock at learning that her husband's anxiety over their little girl's absence was as keen as her own — for Clive was always so calm and level-headed, and if he regarded it as serious enough to go to the police, it meant he really must believe something had happened. And then again, to drag the police into one's home life cannot but be repugnant.

There was nothing actually alarming about Sergeant Tenby, but policemen never seem quite like other men. Their very ordinariness is somehow gruesome.

The Merrimans seated themselves nervously to one side of the table and at the opposite end, a decent businesslike distance away, sat the policeman, his notebook open before him. He began by taking down a description of the little girl.

'Full name: Helen Jennifer Merriman. Age: nine and a half. Height: four feet two inches. Build: slender. Eyes: blue. Hair: long and fair, worn in two plaits.' He drew a line and beneath it wrote: 'Particulars of missing person's apparel when last seen: Blue school blazer and navy pleated skirt, white shirt blouse, red tam o'shanter, white socks and brown shoes.' He glanced up. 'Have you a photograph of her?'

There was a portrait-photograph taken two years ago on her birthday, but the policeman required something more recent — a snapshot would do.

From a drawer in the desk, Mr. Merriman produced an album. To see the sergeant slowly turning the pages while Merriman leaned over his shoulder and pointed out Nell with her brother, Nell pretending to mow the lawn, Nell holding up some small furry animal, they might have been a host politely entertaining a polite guest.

When Tenby had chosen a couple and slipped them between the leaves of his notebook, he leaned back, folded his hands, and said amiably enough, 'And now let us begin from the beginning. What exactly happened, ma'am, when the little girl came home this afternoon?'

Mrs. Merriman moistened her lips. She studied her clasped hands: 'Why, she ran in and asked if she could go to tea with her friend, Sally Cathcart. They're always in and out of each other's houses. I didn't think anything of it. I simply said she wasn't to be late; but she knows quite well that she's not allowed to be out by herself after dark,'

'She came home to dinner at midday as usual?'

'Yes.'

'Was she in trouble with you — or her father? Or at school?'

Mrs. Merriman, astonished, shook her head.

'You believed she was returning to the afternoon session at school as usual?'

Uneasily, Mrs. Merriman ventured to glance at him.

'Of course,' she said.

'You had no idea that she had not gone back?'

'Gone back?' she echoed.

'It seems Nell never went to school this afternoon, Jackie,' said Mr. Merriman, wishing now that he had told her this before; she had gone so white.

She looked incredulously from one to the other. 'But she came home after school! There must be some mistake,' she stammered.

'There was nothing odd about her behaviour that made you the least bit suspicious?'

'No, nothing,' she said with a blank stare. *But what does it mean, what does it mean?* her heart hammered.

'You would have noticed if she had not been herself? She did not strike you as unnaturally excited, say? Or furtive, perhaps?'

'She was a little excited, but I only thought . . . ' Mrs. Merriman recalled the little girl's flushed face and sparkling eyes. 'I only thought,' she went on with difficulty, 'that she was up to something with her friend . . . children's games,' she added hopelessly. She put her hand up to her eyes. The word 'furtive' came back to her mind with odd associations. 'I don't know if it has anything to do with . . . ' she tentatively began. 'Only, last Tuesday Nell was late coming home.' She recalled it quite plainly: Roger was already seated at the tea-table. Where was Nell? she had asked him.

'Dunno,' he answered indifferently, drumming his feet on the chair rail. 'Can I begin? Mum, can I?'

'Didn't you see her when you came out of school?'

The little boy rolled a piece of bread and butter into a telescope, gazed through

22

it at his mother, and then turned it slowly about the room.

'Roger,' she had said patiently.

He came suddenly to himself and crammed the telescope hurriedly into his mouth.

'Roger, did you hear what I said?'

'Yes, Mum,' he said, turning his deceptively open little face towards her. He swallowed and stretched out a small grubby paw for another piece of bread and butter. He came kindly out of his engaging thoughts to say, 'Mum, do you know what? Jimmy's got a real wigwam. It's absolutely super. It's got — '

'Do pay attention, dear. Did Nell say she would be late?'

'No. She didn't say nothing to me. She was talking.'

'*Anything*; she didn't say *anything*, dear. Who was she talking to?' Mrs. Merriman had only meant: which of her schoolfriends? She was totally unprepared for Roger's reply. He was intently examining a sandwich he had broken open, and it was in a preoccupied tone that he mentioned, 'I dunno who it was. Some man.'

'A man,' repeated Mrs. Merriman in a high voice, setting down her cup. 'What man?'

The little boy leaned back in his chair with an air of puffed exhaustion and said in a small voice:

'I don't want any more. Can I go?'

'Finish your tea, there's a good boy,' the mother said automatically.

'I have finished.' Hanging his head to one side, he eyed the food on the table with the nauseated gaze of repletion. 'I don't want any more. I'm full up. I'm bursting. Can I get down? I want to go and play with Jimmy.'

'*May* I get down. Wipe your mouth. I expect the man was someone we know, wasn't he?'

'No,' he had shouted back carelessly as he raced from the room, 'I never seen him before.'

Not long after, Nell had come in and quietly hung up her things in the cloakroom.

'You're late,' her mother had said, as she entered the kitchen.

'Am I?' said the girl, looking round in a

startled way. 'Sorry.'

'What kept you?'

'Nothing,' she replied vaguely, her plaits swinging forward as she bent over her plate. 'I s'pose I just didn't notice the time.'

'Not much use having a watch if you forget to look at it,' her mother observed drily.

'It stopped,' Nell said, covering her wrist quickly with her hand. She looked down. 'I must have forgotten to wind it.'

Mrs. Merriman could still, as it were, 'see' herself standing there under the harsh kitchen light as she ran the iron over a teacloth to test its heat and then spread out one of Nell's school blouses. She had glanced across at the little girl engaged in cutting her bread into small finicky squares, and said casually, 'Who was that man you were talking to?'

Nell's head jerked up round-eyed with amazement. A blush spread over her face. She was staggered by her mother's omniscience. *How did she always know everything?*

'Well?' said her mother.

'I don't know,' she mumbled, bending her head again and quickly putting a piece of bread and butter in her mouth.

'Why were you talking to him, then?'

'I don't know. He — he asked me the way — or something.'

'Was that what made you late? Were you talking to him all this while?'

The child wriggled uneasily on her chair.

'I s'pose so,' she murmured almost inaudibly, taking the opportunity while she thought her mother was not looking to slip her crusts into the saucer behind her cup.

'What was he talking about?' her mother asked casually.

Nell heaved a sigh of enormous fatigue.

'I forget,' she answered vaguely, and swallowed some tea.

'Don't be silly, Nell. How can you have forgotten already?'

'Oh, we talked about school . . . and things,' she replied, wrinkling her brow with the effort of remembrance. 'Nothing partic'lar. Shall I clear away?' she offered innocently, chiefly occupied with the desire to prevent her mother discovering her uneaten crusts.

But her mother demolished that hope abruptly, saying, 'No. I want to talk to you, Nell. You know you've been told a hundred times never to speak to strange men,' she reminded her in a grave voice.

'I didn't, Mummy,' the girl said quickly. 'He spoke to me.'

'There's no need to be pert,' said her mother sharply. 'Daddy and I have told you that you must not speak to strangers. Never mind if they speak to you. You should take no notice.'

'Why?' said Nell, kicking the table leg.

'Oh, my good child,' she had exclaimed in exasperation, meeting the innocent blue stare. 'You're quite old enough to understand these things. Do stop making that noise! There are a great many nasty men about . . . who like to frighten little girls.'

'He wasn't a bit nasty,' Nell declared. 'I liked him. He was jolly nice.'

Her mother banged the iron down so hard that Nell jumped.

'If you're going to be rude and

27

impudent, I shall speak to your father. What *you* need is to go to a good *strict* boarding-school. And *stop* sucking your plait in that disgusting way!'

'What have I done now?' the little girl had cried, jumping from her chair. She broke suddenly into loud sobs. 'You're always picking on me about something . . . I hate you!' She had flung out of the room and clattered upstairs, pretending not to hear her mother calling her to come back.

'You never told me any of this,' said Mr. Merriman, with a troubled frown, when she fell silent.

'You know Nell's little tantrums. I didn't want to bother you with it. It didn't seem of any importance.' She glanced at the sergeant for confirmation.

Sergeant Tenby twiddled his pen between his fingers and said, half to himself:

'What I don't see, is why she came back?'

Mrs. Merriman said stupidly: 'To ask if she might go to tea with Sally.'

'That was the ostensible reason,' he

agreed. 'But we know in fact that she never went.'

'But she must have meant to go,' Mrs. Merriman cried, 'or why should she have taken her paint-box?'

'Her paint-box?'

'She ran upstairs to fetch it. She said she and Sally were going to do some painting.'

'I see.' He made a doodle on the cover of his notebook. 'And did she take it?'

'I suppose so.' She was just a little irritated by this heavy meticulousness, for why on earth should the child have gone upstairs to get it if she had not taken it with her? The one thing her children did *not* do was tell lies.

'It might be as well to find out whether she did take it or not,' the sergeant said casually. He stood up. 'If you wouldn't mind showing me her room . . . '

The paint-box was there, on the table. The first thing they saw as they entered the room.

'But, why . . . ' stammered Mrs. Merriman, very white. 'I don't understand. Why should she . . . ? Please!' she said beseechingly.

Sergeant Tenby said:

'It probably means that she came up to get something else. Will you look and see if anything is missing?'

She glanced round helplessly, but everything swam together. It was Mr. Merriman who discovered it — or, rather, discovered its absence, for he had given it to her himself.

'The pottery pig!' he said, touching the empty place on the chimney shelf. 'That's what she must have taken!'

'A pig!' the sergeant said with a touch of incredulity.

'It was her money-box.'

Mrs. Merriman pressed her knuckles against her mouth. Her husband rested his hand gently on her shoulder (only his awareness of her suffering could have wrung from him such a gesture of physical intimacy before a stranger); he could feel her trembling. 'Steady, dear,' he whispered. She turned her head away.

The sergeant cleared his throat.

'Have you any idea how much there would be in this money-box?'

Merriman said heavily: 'Sixpences . . . an occasional shilling . . . ' and bit his lip, finding it unbearable to think of those few coins so laboriously saved. 'A pound perhaps, altogether,' he muttered.

'I'd like to have a word with the little boy, before I go. He may be able to give us a line on this man you mentioned,' Sergeant Tenby said after a considered moment.

'Now, Sergeant? It's past eleven!'

'If you please. The more information I can get and the sooner I collect it, the easier it will be for us to find her.'

The little boy, stuffed into his dressing-gown all anyhow, flushed with sleep, came blinking into the light.

A voice boomed at him with frightening pleasantry:

'Well, this is a fine time to get you out of bed, young man, isn't it?'

His eyes, with the bright, alert, questioning glance of a robin, roved about the room, taking in his mother's strained unnatural smile; his father, very pale, leaning against the chimney shelf, his head on his hand; and the big burly man standing ominously against the light, his dark uniform seeming to blot up all its brilliance. It was curiously like a dream, in which one senses an oppressive atmosphere without apprehending the cause.

Because it was a frightening dream, he leaned like a baby against his mother's skirt. She put out a hand to him reassuringly and fringed back the dark locks falling over his heated little brow.

'The policeman just wants to ask you a few questions, darling. Don't be afraid,' she murmured.

Towering over him, the man said with immense joviality: 'Enough to make any chap get the wind up, being woken up to talk to a nasty great policeman. But there's nothing to worry about, sonny, we're not carting you off to prison this time.'

As if to verify that this was meant to be a joke, the boy cast a quick anxious glance up to his mother's face.

'Nell hasn't come home, darling; and Mummy and Daddy are worried. This gentleman is helping us to look for her.

He thought you might know . . . that she might have told you something.'

'Why hasn't Nell come home?' he asked in his small clear treble. 'Where is she?'

'Look, sonny,' Sergeant Tenby said persuasively, squatting down to face the little boy, 'remember the other afternoon, your mummy was a bit worried because your sister was late for tea? You saw her talking to a man, didn't you? Had you ever seen him before? No . . . ? Do you remember what he looked like . . . ? Anything at all about him?' He added winningly, 'Now's your chance to be a real detective.'

Roger's eyes slid uneasily away from the great red face so uncomfortably near his own.

'I don't know,' he murmured.

'For instance, was he wearing a hat?'

In a small undecided voice, barely above a whisper, he said, 'I don't think so.'

'Did he have a cap, then?'

The child shook his head, staring at him with round puzzled eyes.

33

'He was bareheaded . . . ? Well, then, that's something.' He patted the boy's shoulder to encourage him. 'Did you notice whether he was fair or dark . . . ? No? Well, never mind. Let's see if you can tell us how he was dressed? Did he look like a workman?'

'I — I don't *think* so.'

'Or was he wearing a suit, perhaps, like your daddy?'

The small hands fidgeted with the red and black cord of his dressing-gown, looping and winding it round his fingers, as he stared at his father; but the fawn suit conveyed nothing to his mind.

'I don't remember,' he said at last, drooping.

'Tall, was he?'

Tall, of course. A silly question.

'How tall? Would you say as tall as Daddy here?'

The little boy heaved a sigh of bewilderment. To someone under four feet, all adults are Brobdingnagian, it is beyond the scope of a small eye to make comparisons of vastness. 'I spy with my little eye' does literally only apply to the minutiae on a level with that small apparatus.

'That's a bit difficult, is it? See if you can answer this one. It would be a help if you could give us some idea what age man he was. Just try, sonny, there's a good chap.'

Roger blinked at the big shining face. He had a confused idea that he was dreaming he was awake; it was like some nightmare lesson in which one had to give the right answer but the questions didn't even make sense.

He said hopefully, 'Seventy?' But that didn't seem right, and he tried again: 'No, forty, I mean . . . ' and heard his mother murmur despairingly, 'They don't understand at that age. He's too young.'

The policeman creaked himself upright with a sigh. In the silence that followed, the little boy sagged against his mother, his elbow digging into her thigh. He was pale with exhaustion. 'Can I go to bed now, Mum?' he mumbled, and laid his head on her lap.

'In just a minute, sonny,' said the policeman from a long way off. He trod slowly across the room and back, tugging at his moustache. Then he came over and crouched by the boy again, holding him steady by a hand on each hip.

'I expect you and Nelly are great pals, eh? Tell each other all sorts of secrets,' the man murmured confidentially.

Roger wondered sleepily who Nelly was.

'He's called Dutchy,' he muttered.

'He's thinking of his rabbit,' Mrs. Merriman said in a soft hopeless voice over his head.

'What's the boy's name?'

'Roger.'

The voices swam dreamily to and fro like water. 'He's half asleep,' someone murmured, and another voice said over and over, 'Poor old chap . . . poor old chap . . . '

'Roger! Wake up!' the policeman ordered in a sudden military voice. The child's head jerked and his lids flew open like a righted doll's. The policeman's face — stern, crimson, wavering — pressed itself before his eyes.

'Roger, listen! Did your sister say

anything to you about running away . . . ? Did she say anything to you about this man you saw her with?'

'Man . . . ' the little boy repeated in a mutter. His lashes drooped, fluttered, drooped . . .

'It's no use,' he heard his mother say, and the misery in her voice tangled into his dreams as he was swept up in his father's arms and carried out of the lighted prison, jogging comfortably up the stairs, asleep before he reached his bed.

* * *

In Nell's opinion, everything was absolutely hateful. She was at that awkward age, stuck — it seemed interminably — in a sort of nowhere between being a mere child and a 'big girl'. That was what they were always saying — 'You're a big girl now' — when they chided her for babyishness. But when it was a question of stopping up late or going to the pictures or deciding what clothes she wanted to wear, then they switched round and declared (just like grown-ups!), 'No, you can't do that! Don't be absurd. You must realize that you're only a little girl.'

There is no boredom to match the resourceless boredom of childhood, a positive physical discomfort. It gave Nell the horrible, rough, restless, chrysalis sensation of no longer fitting properly into her skin. Everything had become so dull and beastly. Everyone was stupid. In a funny sort of way that she could not understand, she had become stupid herself; so that school was a torment to her; since she had moved up to a higher class, she no longer even knew what her lessons were *about*. Her brain seemed to be stuffed with adding, so that there was no longer a crack into which the smallest fact could be crammed. Miss Forrester, her form mistress, was dreadfully scathing. Nell hated her. She sat through class in a fidgety vacuum while the hours dragged by from one subject to the next, punctuated by frantic bells. But being out of school, after the first blissful moment of release, wasn't much better. Games were childish, and her friends were always quarrelling with her. Their tittering excited confidences made her squirm with irritation. She seemed to be the perpetual victim of her own tears and tantrums. She wished she knew what to *do*. She longed to run away and have extraordinary adventures. Nothing interesting ever happened to her.

That man, now, he had been interesting, the way he talked to her, as if she was grownup. Even that had been spoilt by her mother; she spoilt everything. Not that Nell supposed she would ever see him again; it had only been a casual meeting, like grown-ups talking on the corner of the street; that had been part of its charm.

Therefore, as she dawdled down the road to school that afternoon and heard someone calling in a peculiarly soft voice, she spun round like a tee-to-tum to find where the sound came from, and was astounded to see him — the man — sitting on the iron railing separating the pavement from the Common, and beckoning to her.

'Oh! Hullo,' she said, surprised. 'I thought — '

He said in his soft voice, 'I've been waiting for you.'

'For me!' she exclaimed. She went very pink. 'Golly, whatever for — ' she began; and at that moment, to her horror, she remembered her mother's admonition. 'I must go,' she said quickly. 'G'bye.'

'Hey!' he cried, springing from his perch and racing after her. He caught at her flying plait. 'You mustn't run off like that.'

Captured literally by the hairs, she slewed uncomfortably round till she could just see him from the corner of her eye.

'Oh, please,' she said in a panicky voice. 'Do let me go! I'll be late, I'll be late.'

A look of reproach came over his face. He relinquished his grasp on the plait, smooth and cold in his hand as a snake.

'That's not a very nice way to behave, when I've been hanging about for you all this time,' he said reprovingly.

She flushed and tugged her tammy into place.

'I didn't mean to be rude,' she said, glancing to either side, in case there should be anyone to see her talking to this forbidden person; but the road was empty all the way along. 'I'm sorry,' she went on politely, 'but I can't stay now or I shall be late for school.' She banged her satchel nervously against her legs as she spoke.

He tucked his pipe between his lips and considered her for a moment. 'Mind you don't hurt the pigskin,' he remarked.

She glanced down, surprised, at her battered satchel.

'The *pigskin*,' he said, pointing with his pipe-stem at her bare legs.

The *pigskin*! Oh, the pigskin! She had never heard anything so funny. She stumbled about, helpless with mirth.

The man gave a high excited laugh, watching her.

'Oh, I could tell you lots of jokes,' he said eagerly. 'Shall we walk along together?'

She sobered at once into agitation.

'Oh, no, please!' she cried. 'You

mustn't, honestly. I'll get into such trouble!'

He took her hand in his, gently crushing together the soft bones.

'Dear little girl, what is it? What is the matter? Tell me.'

Tears came to her eyes.

She blurted out: 'I've been forbidden to talk to you.' She began to sob a little with excitement. 'Mummy found out — I don't know how . . . I got into an *awful* row . . . She said I mustn't ever . . . ever . . . '

He couldn't catch the gulped words.

'Mustn't ever what, dear?'

'Speak to strange men,' she blubbed. 'She said something terrible would happen to me if I did.'

She wiped her nose with the back of her hand, became aware of a curious silence, and looked up. The man had gone very white, except for his eyes and the tip of his nose which were red, as if he was going to cry.

'How *can* people . . . ? How can they . . . ? Wicked! Wicked!' he stammered. 'People with minds like that shouldn't have children. It's a sin. They're not fit. Here are you — a little child with a soul like a flower — and then your mother, your own mother, fills your head with these filthy thoughts, corrupting your beautiful innocence. It's vile! Vile! It's more than I can bear, to think she should have a child like you.' He clasped her upturned wondering face between his hands and exclaimed with passion: 'Ah, my God, if you belonged to me!'

Nell was deeply excited by this display of emotion. The idea that she was a special sort of person, rare and lovable, and that it was not she, but her mother, who was wicked, thrilled her with its originality.

She said with sycophantic eagerness, 'I told her you weren't a nasty man; I said you were jolly nice,' and added with a shrug, 'She was absolutely furious. She sent me to bed.'

'You poor little kid!' he said, and there were tears in his eyes.

'I didn't care,' she said brashly. 'I don't care if they do send me to boarding-school. I shall run away.' She pivoted round on one heel so that her pleated skirt swung out prettily. 'I often think of running away,' she said with a careless laugh.

'Do you? Do you really, you little darling? I can't say I'm surprised. I expect you feel it would serve them right.'

'Ho, they wouldn't mind! I expect they'd be glad. They hate me really. Well, not Daddy so much, but Mummy does. She only cares about Roger. It doesn't matter what he does, she never gets angry with *him*.' She suddenly abandoned her air of cynicism and said, with a sideways glance of solemnity, 'As a matter of fact, I don't believe she is my mother really. I often think they just adopted me, you know, and that's why she's so unkind.'

'Yes. No wonder you feel like that. It's terrible to be misunderstood. Nothing worse. Don't I know!' he said with a twisted smile. 'I've been through it too. All my life! Let us go and sit over there, and you shall tell me all about it.'

But he went too fast. His suggestion reawakened her uneasy conscience.

'Oh, no, I must go,' she cried, dancing

up and down with anxiety. 'I shall be *late*.'

'It's later than you think,' he observed. 'You're already late, terribly late.'

'Oh, my goodness, am I? Whatever shall I do?' Her eyes were quite round with consternation.

'Don't look so scared,' he said. 'What do they do to you if you're late?'

'Oh, Miss Forrester!' Nell flapped a hand in front of her face and blew out her cheeks. 'I haven't even got an *excuse*.' She had been slowly backing away from him in the manner of one in the presence of royalty, preparing to turn with a jaunty wave and fly off, when the thought of having to explain what had kept her struck her with dismay. 'Oh, crummy!' she whispered.

'What would they do if you didn't go at all? They couldn't do anything, could they? Well, then? Doesn't it strike you that our meeting like this might be of more importance to you than a school lesson?' He watched from the corner of his eye the indecision plain on the small face. 'You know — what did you say your name was? — oh, yes, Nell . . . you know that I came all the way back specially to see you again.'

'To see me?'

'Yes. I've thought about you so much.'

She came a few steps nearer. He was absorbed in stuffing tobacco into his pipe, deliberately taking no notice of her, as if it was a small bird or a wild animal he wished to tame.

He said, 'You struck me as such a splendid little kid.'

'Did I?' she murmured shyly, turning very pink, as he paused to suck his pipe alight.

'There was something about you that appealed to me. Perhaps because I'm lonely too.'

Something stirred inside her, began to beat rapidly, like wings fluttering in her breast.

'There's something in me that feels very close to you. Do you feel it too?'

'I don't know,' she said awkwardly.

'Ah, it is because you are a little girl and I am a man that it sounds strange to you; but it is your soul speaking to mine.

And that is why it *sickens* me,' he said with passionate emphasis, going white under the eyes, 'to think of you becoming fouled all over by other people's obscene ideas.' He spat the words out as if they were poison.

She watched his face working, faintly embarrassed by his intensity and yet fascinated that herself was the cause of his agitation.

He was trembling uncontrollably, as if he was going to fall. He turned without a word and walked away from her across the Common with a curious stiff gait.

She was afraid that he was angry with her. She ran after him and put her hand into his. He said nothing, did not look down at her, simply held her hand tightly and pressed it to him, against his heart.

After a moment, he said, a trifle hoarsely:

'I'm sorry, dear. I shouldn't let myself get so easily upset. Be patient with me. Try and understand.'

'Oh, I do,' she said fervently. 'I often get upset myself.'

'You're wonderful,' he said, catching

her other hand and swaying them to and fro, 'a wonderful little kid!' He blinked tears from his lashes. 'I really do believe that if anyone could understand, you could.'

The child blushed with pleasure.

'If I had someone like you, I'd never be lonely again,' he said. 'What a little pal you'd be to a chap. We'd have such good times together. I can just imagine the two of us, tramping the world together. Would you like that?'

'Oh, I would,' she breathed.

'Ah, don't I wish it were possible! But it would never do, my dear; they'd never let us. Besides, I live too rough. You'd never be able to stick it. It's too adventurous a life for a girl.'

'I *love* adventures,' she protested. 'It's what I always want. And I really am awfully strong. Truly. Oh, couldn't we? I can climb trees, and I've got my woodcraft badge. I'd be *useful*, I really would.'

'Of course you would, bless your plucky little heart. Do you think I don't know that? Why, just to have you with me would fill me with such courage . . . ' He dropped down in sudden exhaustion to the rough turf, and said in a defeated tone: 'It wouldn't do, my child.'

She knelt beside him.

'Why wouldn't it do? Why wouldn't it?'

'A foolish dream of happiness, that's all it was,' he said bitterly. 'Do you read your Bible? Do you remember Cain? A homeless wanderer on the face of the earth!' A sick look came over his face and he shuddered. 'I must get on,' he said. 'It was a mistake to come back. I thought that by doubling back on my tracks I could shake them off. Try to imagine what it's like to feel yourself surrounded by enemies — faceless enemies. It's like walking in perpetual darkness, never knowing when one may fall into some pit in the ground. There's not a living soul in all the world I dare trust.'

'You could trust me,' she said stoutly.

'Yes. I could trust you,' he said, bending his eyes to conceal the sudden tears. She said tentatively:

'If I was with you, I could help you look out for them. They wouldn't expect to see me, and it might make them think you were someone else. We could disguise ourselves too,' she went on, sparkling with enthusiasm, her mind enchanted with the prospect of adventures, danger, excitement, plotting against the plotters, and dressing-up.

A stout woman with a shopping basket crossed the Common and stared at them curiously as she passed. Nell made an ugly face at her retreating back.

'What's she want to stare at us like that for?'

An agitated expression crossed the man's face.

'Do you think she recognized me?' he muttered, and scrambled to his feet, patting his clothes straight. 'I must go.'

Nell, squatting on the grass, turned her face up to him with a pleading look.

'Let me come with you.'

'I don't know, I don't know,' he said distractedly. 'We can't stay here any longer. It isn't safe.'

The child jumped to her feet.

'Do you mean it? Truly? Will you take me?'

He took the little face between his hands and subjected it to a long, sad scrutiny.

'Are you sure you really want to come?'

'Oh, I do, I do!' She flung herself on him. 'Oh, you are kind! I do love you!' Embracing his waist, she tipped her head back and looked up at him. 'You know my name, but you never told me yours.'

He stared up at the sky in thought.

'You can call me George.'

'Just George? That's like real friends, isn't it?' she exclaimed with satisfaction.

They were nearly at the far side of the Common when she heard the church clock chime the quarter and a sudden thought struck her.

'Is that quarter to four? They'll be coming out of school.' Her face lit up: 'I must go home.'

'Home!' he said in consternation. 'You can't go home now, if you want to come with me. I thought you meant it when you asked me to take you along. I thought I had found someone absolutely sincere. If it was only a game you'd better run along quick. I've no time for little hypocrites.'

'I did mean it. I did.' She was almost in tears. 'I only want to go home *first*. To fetch something. Something important. Something I want to take with me. A surprise.'

He regarded her gravely, still too shaken to be quite convinced.

'And suppose someone should see you and ask what you are up to, what will you say?'

She sent him a glance radiant with mischief.

'Don't you *see*? It's just because school is over that it's all right for me to go. Mummy will be *expecting* me. And I shall tell her that Sally has asked me to tea. She's my friend and I often go there. If Mummy thinks I'm with her, she won't miss me for *hours*. It'll be much more fun.'

But he did not smile back at her. He could feel the fragile little bones in her thin shoulders. He drew her to him and gazed down into the candid eyes.

'You wouldn't play me false and betray

me to them, would you?'

She stared at him solemnly.

'I swear, George. Slit my throat if I tell a lie!'

His face turned a mottled red.

'*What* did you say?'

'It's an oath,' she said, gazing at him in astonishment. 'A solemn oath. *See that wet, see that dry* — ' She licked a small pink finger and held it up for him to see. ' — *you may slit my throat if I tell a lie.*'

When Nell came back with the pottery pig jingling in her hand, the man was lying on his face beneath a clump of bushes: so still, so limp, that for a horrible moment she thought he was dead . . . He *looked* dead. Like a dead tramp sprawling there. She said, 'George!' in a quavering voice. After a moment, he stirred, groaned, and rolled languidly over onto his back.

'I was asleep,' he said. 'I've had no sleep for nights.' He sat up. 'Hullo, you're back!'

'I've got it,' she cried, shaking the pottery pig at him.

His jacket was unbuttoned, and as he sat up it fell open.

'Oh! Whatever have you been doing? You *have* made your shirt dirty!'

He buttoned the jacket quickly across the ugly brownish patches on his woollen shirt.

'It's nothing,' he said.

There were stains splashed over his trousers too, she now saw, stiff and dark, like dried blood.

'Did you have a nosebleed?' she enquired with interest. 'Poor you, you must have bled like anything.' She said, with a little air of housewifeliness, 'You ought to get it washed out or it will leave a mark.'

'It's nothing,' he said again. 'Just old clothes, not worth bothering about. Marks like these . . . never . . . ' He fell silent and then added: 'I'll get some new ones and throw these away.' Looking whitish, exhausted, he stretched out a hand for the pig.

'What's in here?' he said, rattling it.

'Money!' she exclaimed with delight. 'It's for you, George.'

'My dear little kid, I wouldn't take your money!'

'But I want you to. It's for our travels.'

He was moved almost to tears.

'What a little brick you are! I love you for that. And I'll never forget you offered it to me. Your precious savings . . . ' He bent and printed a light kiss on her forehead, pressing her hands once more round the fat pink pig. 'Come on,' he said. 'We've a long way to go before nightfall.'

'Where are we going?' she asked, skipping along at his side.

'We'll make our way south,' he said, and as they walked he elaborated a fantastic plan: first to reach a port, then to find a ship where he could work his passage and smuggle her aboard, a ship that would take them to some far country where the sun always shone and there were monkeys, bananas, and coconuts, and an unending series of splendid adventures, culminating in the discovery of a marvellous hidden city in the jungle, full of buried treasure, where they would live for ever, and he would be king and she would be his queen.

Once they stopped at a wayside café for mugs of steaming milky coffee and buns. He took a bagful of buns and sliced ham away with them, to eat another time.

It was perhaps an hour later that Nell said in a small voice:

'Is it much further, George?'

'Tired?'

'I think I'm getting a blister on my heel.'

'Then we'll stop.' He looked about him. 'This seems to be as good a place as any to find shelter. Sure to be a barn somewhere.' He lifted her onto a stone wall beside the path. 'You wait there, old dear, while George goes off to find somewhere we can sleep. I won't be long.'

Westward, crimson burned through the latticed trees. The fields turned dark as violets and from the dense charcoal shadows crept a thready white mist. Tiny lights sprang up one after another in the distance, as if people were striking matches in the gloom. She shrank when a car, its headlights glaring, roared past her like a wild animal in the dusk.

The little girl had felt so utterly safe with George that it was only now, his reassuring presence gone, that she began to be frightened. There were funny noises, little quiet ones, as though a ghost was creeping up behind her. *Suppose, just suppose, George never comes back? Suppose I have to stay here alone all night?* The town child thought with horror of spiders and worms and a hundred other crawling things. There, all round her, lay the unknown countryside. She was miles and miles from home and she didn't even *know* where she was. She was *lost*. Suppose she could *never find her way back*, and was lost for ever?

She sprang off the wall, grazing her knees on the rough stone, and began to run screaming down the road:

'George ... George ... *Wait for me ... I'm coming TOO ...* '

★ ★ ★

It was useless to keep asking the sergeant, 'What do you think can have happened to her?' Mrs. Merriman knew there was no answer he could give. Yet the question uttered itself hopelessly again and again. Fantastic ideas ranged through her mind, to be superseded by the more literal horrors of the child lying out on the Common somewhere with a broken leg, or having tumbled into the pond and drowned among the rushes and scummy water-plants. Such thoughts made this impotent waiting intolerable. She needed to rush into the night and search in all the places her imagination presented to her, to run across the Common calling, to pass through twenty streets at once and peer down every suspect alley. Nothing could really satisfy her desperate heart but to know that the entire police force was beating the bushes and flashing its torches into black doorways. So much time being wasted in futile questioning was agony. Easier for Clive to endure it, for like all men he trusted in method and reason and the logical approach; he held to the idiotic belief that the longest way round was the quickest way home. But not, she cried to herself in protest, when one's child is lost and God knows where

... The not knowing ... The not knowing ...

When at last Sergeant Tenby rose to go, she turned from her pacing to ask what he was going to do.

'I shall go back to the station and make my report.'

'But I mean, what are you going to *do*? Where are you going to look for her? How do you set about it?' Only the extreme of anguish could have wrung such boldness, such bluntness from her.

He said equably:

'This information — ' He tapped his breast-pocket where his notebook was. ' — is sent to all stations in the vicinity. Every policeman on duty will have her description and will be on the lookout for her. The public will be asked to report anything they know which may be concerned with the little girl's disappearance. Etcetera,' he added, like a full stop. One had to be canny about just how much one told. To a person half-deranged with anxiety, a word too much, a word too explicit, could alarm rather than soothe.

The woman said wildly:

'But aren't you going to *do* anything? Aren't you even going to search for her? My God, what is the use of just waiting till she turns up somewhere? Suppose she never — ' Mrs. Merriman broke off. Not even in her distress could she dare to finish the sentence; a natural superstitious terror forbade it. Superstition would willingly have banished the thought from her mind too, if it could; the thought *Suppose she is already dead*, and the dreadful little picture that accompanied it of a child half buried under fallen leaves.

'Don't you worry, ma'am, you can trust us to deal with the matter properly. It's naturally an anxious business for you, but the police handle cases like this all the time. I daresay you'd be surprised to learn of the hundreds of missing persons who are reported to us in a year that we trace.'

Mrs. Merriman was too afraid of antagonizing him to say *What about the ones you don't find?*, thinking of the blurred little photographs of smiling children year after year in the public prints; discovered — horribly — mutilated, ravished, dead . . .

Her face was white, glistening with fatigue.

'We must get the BBC to broadcast an SOS!' she said.

Sergeant Tenby said calmly:

'We'll hope that won't be necessary, ma'am.'

On the doorstep, he said in a low voice to Merriman, 'Take my advice, sir, and get your good lady to bed with a hot drink and something to make her sleep, if you've got it. It won't do her any good to wait up for the kiddy to come back tonight.'

But when Merriman returned from the front door, Mrs. Merriman had already huddled on her old coat and was groping in a blind sort of way along the shelf in the cloakroom, among the odd gloves and galoshes, for a torch. The torch clattered down and his hand reached it a second before hers. But she held on to it.

'Let me have it, Clive. I'm going to look for her.'

'Now, Jackie! Dear, listen to me.' He

61

could not bear to tell her it wouldn't be any use. He stroked her hair. 'You're so tired,' he said.

Her eyes flashed wetly as she shook her head.

'I must. I must find her. Clive, don't you see, that policeman's no good. They don't understand. To them it's just another . . . But it's our little girl. She may be out there somewhere now . . . needing me . . . at this very moment . . . calling . . . '

'I know. I know,' he murmured, rocking her in his arms. 'But I don't want you to go just yet; you're not fit. If you'll wait a moment, I'll knock up the woman next door and ask her to sit in with Roger, and then we can go together.'

But she wasn't listening. Or rather, she was listening to something else.

'Is that Roger? I think he's awake. Go and see what he wants, Clive.'

Deceived by this feint, he had hardly turned the corner of the stairs when she stole across the kitchen and slipped out of the side door. He ran downstairs.

'*Jackie*!'

He went after, following the staggering torch-beam. She was weeping in the darkness and calling 'Nell ... Nell ... Nell!' It frightened him to hear her, this woman always so composed and so quiet. He did eventually manage to persuade her home. He thought: *The policeman was right, she'll have to have something to make her rest.* And he went and phoned the doctor. While he was in the call-box, it occurred to him to phone Jacqueline's sister. He listened to the phone whirring, whirring. When he had almost given up hope, the receiver clicked.

'Win? It's Clive,' he said.

'Clive! Good God! Do you know what the time is?'

'Yes. I'm sorry.'

'What's happened?' she said quickly.

'It's Nell. We've lost her,' he said in a dull voice, too weary to think what he was saying.

There was a moment's complete silence. Then she said: 'It's not possible! How ... ?'

'No! I didn't mean ... Oh, no! Not

that. I meant, we've *lost* her. She's been gone all day. We don't know where she is.' He cut short her futile questions. 'Look, Win, I can't stop long. I haven't any more money, for one thing, and I must get back, I'm waiting for the doctor . . . for Jackie. She's nearly demented. Well, you can imagine. I wondered if you could possibly come over for a . . . just to help us through — the waiting. Jackie oughtn't to be alone.'

The pips broke across.

Winifred cried through them: 'I'll come if I can. I'll have to get leave. Try not to — ' and the line went dead.

It was half past two when he got back to the house, and she was washing the kitchen paint. She had taken all the china off the dresser and was cleaning it down.

He clasped the back of her neck tenderly.

He said, 'Come to bed, old girl. Look, I'm dead beat, and I've got to go to work tomorrow. I can't go to bed and leave you down here. Come up with me, there's a good girl.'

'You go. I'm all right,' she muttered. 'I

want to finish this. I couldn't sleep.'

The doctor, when he arrived, appeared to think that was quite reasonable. She would naturally want to stay awake in case there was any news, he said. But this pill wasn't to make her *sleep*, it was just to steady her nerves; for she'd had a bad shock, she must remember. It would be better for her to lie down for a little after taking it, otherwise it might make her giddy.

So they got her upstairs and into bed. Clive fell asleep with his arm across her, and woke uneasily a few hours later to find her gone. She was downstairs, sitting in her dressing-gown by the dead fire, her eyes wide with the strain of listening for sounds that never came, the knuckles of her thin hands locked tightly together as if in prayer.

★   ★   ★

It is alarming to wake in the dark to see that the wall beneath one's bedroom window and the window itself have vanished — blown, it would appear, clean away, leaving a big square cavity, not filled with the quiet familiar line of roofs one expected to see, but crowded instead with lean trees reaching out twisted black branches against the night sky. It gave one an awful upside-down feeling — for a moment. It was more bewilderment than wide-awake panic, like the vague uncertainty of one's identity as one lies sluggish between two states of consciousness. And then the spiky straw against one's bare legs brought it all back to mind in a rush of astonishment.

This was The Adventure. She had actually run away from home, exactly like some plucky schoolgirl in a storybook. Nell the Intrepid Girl-Explorer, she thought with rapture, sleeping out in a barn. The wonder of it amazed her. It wouldn't even surprise her after this if in the end she did turn out to be a princess, stolen in her cradle by wicked gipsies and sold to her parents.

It is said that one cannot think of more than one thing at a time, but thoughts go so fast that it sometimes seems as if one can. Even while Nell dreamed she was entertaining her mother and father in her palace with its walls of mother-of-pearl, the slivers of straw pricking her flesh made her wonder again, as she flinched and shifted uneasily, how the Little Mermaid (herself a sort of princess) could have borne to put her foot to the ground when every step was a knife cutting into her. She was aware at the same time that the night was full of noises. Something scampered over the iron roof ... Thumping ... Scuffling ... And something uttered a terrible lost cry.

A bird, she hoped; but all the same, she kept her eyes on the opening in case Something — unmentionable and shapeless — should appear with eyes glowing like cigarette ends. *Red* eyes were the worst. There had once been a witch she had heard of with red eyes that shone in the dark ... But that was not something to be thought of at night.

The eye, when she saw it, was pale and brilliant, gleaming through the bushes at her. Rigid and sweaty-cold, Nell stared back. For a long time, Nell watched the eye watching her through the shaking leaves. Her heart was racing.

With an enormous effort of courage, she did at last manage to cry out in a shaky whisper: 'George!'

Instantly, from some distance behind her, came his nice calm voice:

'Hullo, there! Aren't you asleep?'

'I'm frightened,' she shamefully quavered, and a tear ran down her nose.

He had been lying comfortably on his back, his arms under his head, and his empty pipe dangling onto his chest; but at her tearful voice he came over and, sitting on a bale of straw, took her onto his knee.

'What is it, you funny little mutt?'

'Something out there, watching me. I don't like it,' she said, pressing her face into his stuffy shirt. She could feel his heart bumping.

'What's it like?' he said in a level voice.

'An eye,' she gabbled into his chest. 'In the bushes.'

After a moment, he said:

'I see it.'

George was so nice. He didn't laugh at her or call her a silly baby; he just showed her that what had frightened her was a light in the darkness, shining through the leaves as they swayed to and fro. Once it had been explained to her, she could see it for herself, of course. She gave a shamefaced giggle.

George said there was nothing for her to be afraid of while she was with him; he would never let any harm come to her. With his arm round her she did feel perfectly safe; safe enough, even though it was as dark as a cave in the barn, to ask what he would have done if it had been an eye out there, an eye belonging to some beastly Thing all boneless and horrible and without a proper face. But the idea didn't scare George in the least; he knew just how to kill those awful jellyish creatures: you went for the eye, their one vulnerable point; you drove the knife right in to the hilt and turned it; the blood came out thick and black, and they were dead in a minute.

The blade glittered faintly in the light from the doorway as he stabbed the air with it to show her the peculiar twisting movement he would use.

She gave a delicious shudder. 'Is it sharp?'

'Sharp enough to split a hair.'

'Would it really kill someone?'

'That's what it's for,' he said. He tilted up her face and looked at her gravely. 'Did you remember to say your prayers?'

She clapped a hand to her mouth. 'Oh, dear!'

'Better say them now.' He tumbled her off his knee, and she knelt obediently in the straw and bowed her head over her joined hands. When she had finished, he asked suddenly in a queer voice if she had prayed for him too, and seemed strangely relieved to learn that she had . . .

The knife jagging into her eye, making her heart beat with terror — and she couldn't push it away because George had her hands in his — turned out to be a beam of sunlight prying into the corner of her sleep-shut eye. George did indeed have her hands in his and was trying to hoick her to her feet.

'Sun up, old lady! Show a leg!'

'Oh, George, I thought — ' she began, but he cut her short.

'Briskly does it. We've got to clear out, quick, before anyone comes.' He brushed the wisps of straw from her rumpled clothes. 'Look what I've got for our breakfast,' he said, as she staggered about on one leg fastening her shoes, and held up two eggs in triumph; 'What do you think of that?'

'But, George,' she said after a moment, 'how are we going to cook them?'

'Boil 'em,' said George.

'But what I mean is, *how*? What in?'

'You'll see.'

She hopped along at his side. The morning was crisp and bright. Dew lay like frost on the grass, sparkling violet and red where the sun struck it. It was wonderfully pretty. As they walked along the road, George suddenly darted with noiseless steps up a little path leading to the back of a cottage, lifted the lid of a dustbin, and began poking about inside. He came back with a battered old saw-edged can that had once contained baked beans.

'What's that for?' she asked, wrinkling her nose.

'Our saucepan,' he said, stooping to rinse it out in the stream that ran in the ditch beside the road. He half-filled it with water and, with the twigs she had collected, laid a neat little fire. His ingenuity delighted her; she had no doubt that he was just about the cleverest man in the world. When the fire was going nicely, he slipped the eggs carefully into the can and set it on the red-hot heart.

Stale buns and hard-boiled eggs could never have tasted more delicious. Birds flashed overhead. Somewhere out of sight, a lark was scratching out his song against the sky. George said it was a lark. George knew about such things. He lay on one elbow, the smoke from his pipe ascending lazily into the air, and in his soft voice identified the birds winging past them, showed her a rabbit darting across the bottom of the field — a thing she had never seen before. Indeed, he seemed to know the meaning of everything he saw.

She could have stayed there forever listening to him. It gave her quite a pang when he stamped out their dear little fire and said it was time to shift.

★   ★   ★

About noon of that day, a woman pushed open the door of the police station and marched into the bleak little office. A constable writing at the tall desk that divided the room like a counter looked up.

'Yes, madam?'

She said aggressively, 'I want to see someone; the inspector, I suppose.'

'What's it about, if you please?'

Well, then, if it's any business of YOURS, she as good as said, but didn't. 'It's about the little girl who's disappeared.'

The constable slipped into the next room and closed the door behind him. He came back in a few minutes to say that the sergeant would see her.

'Good morning,' said Sergeant Tenby pleasantly. 'Will *you* sit down? You wished to see me?'

She stood there.

'I don't know so much.'

'I beg your pardon?'

'He said you were a sergeant. I want to see the inspector.'

'I'm afraid the inspector's out. If it's not important, perhaps you'd care to call back some other time.'

'It is important — or it may be. That's why I wanted to see someone like an inspector or a superintendent.'

'I see.' Sergeant Tenby leaned back in his chair with an expression at once bland and unhelpful.

She stood there uncertainly.

'Oh, well,' she decided, 'you'll have to do. I haven't the time to waste back and forthing.' She bumped down on to the chair and heaved her basket onto her lap. 'It was only on the off-chance I came, not knowing whether it would be useful or not.'

'Your name, please,' he said, licking a finger and pulling a thin sheet of paper towards him.

'Now, look,' the woman said, 'I don't want to be mixed up in this, it's nothing to do with me. I mean, I'm not going to be a witness, or any of that stuff.'

She pushed her hat to the back of her head. 'Mrs. Perrott,' she said sulkily, and watched him write it at the top of the page.

'And the business?'

She looked at him affronted, though his head was bent over the paper. This was just what she expected of the police; it was as bad as going to the doctor, the things they wanted to know.

'I'm not in business, as it happens. I'm a housewife.'

'I refer, of course, to the matter you have come to see me about.'

'I told your man in there. Didn't he tell you? It's about that little girl who's supposed to have disappeared.'

'What little girl?' he mildly inquired.

'Don't you know about it yet? It was this friend of mine who told me I ought to come to the police. Not much use me mentioning it, if you're not in the know.'

'I can't know which child you're referring to unless you tell me, can I?' he said reasonably.

'You got so many missing girls in these parts, then?'

Defeated, he said, 'Do you mean Helen Merriman?'

'How should I know?' she argued bewilderingly. She countered, 'The girl's a stranger to me.'

'Yes, I see,' he said at last with a gentle sigh. 'Perhaps the best way would be for you to tell me what you know, and leave me to sort it out afterwards.'

She looked at him sideways, suspiciously; rummaged in her basket, as if her story was tucked in there among the parcels, and began defensively, 'Of course, it may not have anything to do with this child who's disappeared. It was my friend, Mrs. Ramsey, who thought I ought to come and tell you about it. I was talking to her in The Blue Teapot this morning. I drop in there most days for a coffee. And we were chatting, my friend and I, and she happened to mention that her neighbour's little girl was lost. So I was asking her about it, the way one does. I mean, it's a terrible thing, isn't it? And she said how it seemed this child hadn't gone to school as usual, and there they were, the parents, waiting and waiting for her to come home, and she never came. Well, it was her saying that about her not going to school that reminded me. I said, 'Why, I saw a child in school uniform yesterday afternoon; I wonder if it was her?' And Mrs. Ramsey, she said, if it was it might be important, and I should go and tell the police right away.'

Sergeant Tenby said, 'I'll have Mrs. Ramsey's address, if you please.'

Mrs. Perrott bridled.

'*She* doesn't know anything about it, but what I told her.'

He said patiently, 'You said Mrs. Ramsey was a neighbour of the people whose child is missing. If I know where she lives I shall be able to tell whether we're discussing the same case, won't I?'

She had to give him best there.

She said, 'She lives in Park Avenue, at Sunny Nook. And the other people live in a house called 'Jacqmancote'. I've always noticed it when I've been going to see Mrs. Ramsey, because it's such a funny name for a house, isn't it?'

He made a sound of agreement.

'Where did you say you saw the little girl?'

'I didn't say, did I?' she said. You had to be sharp with the police, they were only looking to catch you out if they could. 'It was on the Common. I was on my way back from the shops.'

'What time would that be?'

'About three, I should think. I wouldn't have been gone all that long, I only went to the butcher. And it can't have been half-past, because that's what made me look at her — being in school uniform, you see. I said to myself, 'And what are you doing out of school at this hour, miss?''

'And what was she doing?'

'Good gracious, I don't know!' the woman said irritably. 'I didn't *ask* her. It wasn't any of my business.'

'I mean, was she playing? Was she walking as if she was on her way somewhere? Was she, for instance, by herself?'

'No, she wasn't.' Mrs. Perrott said triumphantly. 'She was with a man. They were sitting on the grass together. I must say, it struck me as peculiar.'

'Yes? Now, why was that?'

'The man was peculiar.'

'Oh, he was? In what way?'

That was difficult to define. She ran a finger over the fancy stitching on the back of her glove while she considered.

'It didn't seem natural to see them together, somehow. I thought to myself, 'Well, I don't know who you may be, but I'll bet you're not her Dad'.' She nodded her satisfaction.

The sergeant wove an elastic band round his fingers.

'Now, I wonder what made you think that. Can you go back in your mind and try to remember what gave you that idea?'

'I can't say really. He was sort of odd-looking, I suppose.' She frowned. 'He had a kind of nervous way of looking round. I don't know. There was something about him. I can't explain. But that must have been why I noticed them; and then, when my friend mentioned about this little girl going off, I remembered.'

'This little girl, would you know her again, do you think?'

The woman pulled her hat forward over her brow and pushed it to the back of her head again, flustered to find how vague the image was now she came to look.

'I might.'

'Was she fair or dark?'

She said haughtily, 'I'm afraid I didn't take all that much notice.' That was always the way it was: you did your best to help people, and then just because you couldn't answer every little question, they wouldn't believe anything. 'What I do remember is that she was wearing the school blazer and red tammy.'

Sergeant Tenby leaned sideways and took a file out of a drawer, leafing through the photographs inside. He picked out half a dozen and pushed them across the desk.

'See if you can identify her among these.'

She went through them slowly.

'This one looks as if it might be her,' she said at last. 'Or this one.'

'Yes?' he said with a carefully expressionless face, and scooped them up. 'And the man? Can you give me a description of him?'

'He turned his face away, as if he didn't want me to see him. He had this untidy hair — blowing about, rather — sort of dun colour. Or it might have been brown going grey. Quite a clean-looking person, he was: what you'd call fresh-complexioned, I suppose. I couldn't really tell his height, as he was sitting down, but I should guess him to be tallish — ' She looked at the man opposite. ' — though not as broad as you. He had on grey flannels and a dark sort of jacket — navy, I think. Oh, and I fancy he was wearing a grey shirt. Quite ordinary and respectable, he seemed; I mean, he didn't look common or anything like that.'

'And yet he did seem to you peculiar.'

'Yes, he did,' she said defiantly, 'and it's no good asking me why, because I don't know. It was just something about him.'

'What did you think he was, may I ask? Did he look like a crook, for instance?'

'How should I know what a crook looks like?' she demanded. 'But if you're so keen to know what I thought,' she added scornfully, 'I thought he looked batty.'

* * *

'It looks as though we may have got a line on the Merriman girl, sir,' Tenby said when his superintendent came back. He handed him the notes. 'Of course,' he went on, as the superintendent turned the pages, 'I hardly expected the woman to identify her from that snapshot. The girl was wearing a tammy when she saw her, and that would be bound to make a difference. It's not much of a description of the man either, I'm afraid, but what struck me was how she kept saying there was something odd about the bloke, and at last she said he looked batty.' He paused. 'I wondered, what about that chap who escaped from Finmore Park Mental Hospital last week? So far as we know, he hasn't turned up anywhere. It's just as likely that he might have made his way down here. He'd naturally be trying to get as far away as he could, I suppose. Wouldn't you think, sir?'

'It's not what I want to think,' said Superintendent Marlowe.

'Sir?'

'You haven't any children, have you, Tenby?' he said drily. He grated back his chair and crossed to the window, where he stood looking into the yard. He said, 'Tell them to get me Finmore Park on the phone; I want to speak to the Medical Officer.' He waited, drumming blunt fingers on the pane. It was not that he was an imaginative man, nor a sentimental one; it was rather that he had too much experience and did not care to think what might have happened to the child if she had been picked up by a lunatic, one of those sex-maniacs only too probably. And girl children always reminded him of the small girl of his own that he had lost many years ago. No, not lost; 'lost' was a tiresome euphemism for grief; his little girl had simply gone from them, slipped away through the last door of all.

He picked up the telephone, and said

in a tired voice, 'Superintendent Marlowe of the Metropolitan Police speaking. It's about the male patient who escaped from your hospital last week . . . Yes, Leonard Wheedler, that's the one. Have you any news of him . . . ? We've a report on a man down here who seems to answer the description . . . No, we haven't got him. He was seen talking to a little girl, who subsequently went missing from her home.'

The medical officer was not helpful. He seemed afraid of committing himself to a direct answer, quibbling over terminology with the exasperating pedantry of a semanticist. Marlowe doggedly persisted, and it was almost inadvertently that the doctor mentioned the positive fact that when Wheedler had been admitted to the hospital five years ago, he had been suffering from persecution mania, aggravated by homicidal tendencies.

Marlowe smote the desk with his open hand. He said bitterly, 'A homicidal lunatic! I appreciate your mentioning the fact.'

'It would be a pity to unduly emphasize

the point,' said the doctor. 'It was no more than a tendency, a repressed tendency, of which the patient himself was unaware, and there have been no indications of latent violence for more than three years. However,' he went on, clearing his throat, 'we must hope that the shock and strain he must be under at the present time don't have the effect of reawakening the old aggressive fears.'

'We must indeed,' Marlowe snarled, slamming down the phone.

'No good, sir?' asked Tenby.

Marlowe said acidly, 'I suppose if you spend your life among loonies you must expect to become like them. Well, the girl doesn't stand much chance, if it is Wheedler she's gone off with.' He went over to the map on the wall and stared at it. He jabbed the point of his pencil at the Common, and from there began tracing invisible arcs.

'If the girl is still alive and he's taken her with him, he'll keep on the move, won't he? Even a madman, I suppose, wouldn't be such a fool as to linger in the neighbourhood of the child's home.

We'll have to assume that his mind works on more or less logical lines. If he's been going south all this while, he's not very likely, in my opinion, to turn on his tracks now. He'll keep on keeping on. His main endeavour will be to evade recapture. He may well be out of our manor by now; we'll have to pass this on to the county police. Take down these possible routes,' he said, reading them off the map. 'And if the prints of that snapshot have come in, get them off to the press, together with a description of the man she is believed to be with . . . And, Tenby! Don't give them any hint that we know who the man is. I don't want his identity broadcast, not in connection with the girl; it's too risky. If it gets into the papers, Wheedler might see it and get the wind up, and out of sheer panic try and get rid of the child.' He turned away and added, 'Besides, I'd rather those wretched parents didn't know anything about it; no need for them to have that additional torture.'

* * *

It was torture enough indeed for the Merrimans. It was their helplessness that was so agonizing for them; that, and the blank of unknowing. The best Mrs. Merriman could do to quiet her mind was to engage herself in one task after another, as if the activity of her hands could keep her thoughts at bay. The very ordinariness of scrubbing floors and turning out cupboards was soothing, and could sometimes make the beating clock fade momentarily into silence.

Even when there was no more work to be done, she could not stay still for long; she was driven by an uncontrollable restlessness. She would try to listen to what her sister was saying, but in a minute or two she would recommence her Demeter-like wandering from room to room with an apologetic murmur: 'Don't take any notice of me. I can't help it. I'm sorry. Rotten for you, all this.'

What could Winifred do except trail after her and try to persuade her not to worry? 'You should get some rest, Jackie. You're wearing yourself out. It's not fair on Clive for him to have to worry over you as well.'

Mrs. Merriman's great vacant eyes would fix on her sister's with every appearance of attention. 'Yes,' she would say. 'Yes, I know . . . But why don't the police *find* her? What are they *doing*? She can't have got far, can she?'

Winifred would say stoutly, 'Of course she can't. They'll find her all right, they're bound to find her.' And in an attempt to distract her sister's mind she would brightly narrate some little account of her job or a mutual friend or a play she had seen; but directly she had finished, Mrs. Merriman, her eyes still religiously fastened on her sister's, would once more demand dully, urgently: 'What can have happened to her, Win? Where can she be?'

Yet, though her thoughts constantly wheeled and swooped, soaring away and returning to that dark patch in her mind, like gulls flying around the one delectable putrescence on a stony shore, it was not until the following day that she pecked out a vivifying morsel: that among Nell's classmates there might be one in whom she had confided something of her plans.

It seemed to her senseless and unnatural of Win to try to dissuade her from going down to the school to question them, when it was so obvious that that was what she must do.

The children streamed past them, chattering shrilly and jostling one another, and she scanned the bright-cheeked bobbing faces for those she knew belonged to Nell's class. She plucked at them as they passed: 'You know Nell Merriman, don't you ... ? You know Nell Merriman?'

They stared uneasily at this queer-looking woman, with her funny stretched smile and eyes like glass in their deep bruised sockets, as at something not quite human. One or two of them tittered from pure nervousness. 'Go on, Maureen,' said one child, pushing forward the girl beside her, 'You're a friend of Nell's.'

At this betrayal, Maureen went scarlet and grabbed the wrist of the girl next to her. 'So's Phyllis,' she said. 'And Jean. And ... Rosie.'

They stood in front of the lady, biting

their lips and looking slyly down their noses.

Mrs. Merriman tried to smile at them reassuringly.

'My little girl — ' she began, and could not go on. She put a shaking hand up to her mouth.

Her sister said quickly, 'Do you children know why Nell hasn't been to school the last few days?'

The little girls sought one another's eyes furtively.

Someone at last uttered a strangled negative.

Winifred said:

'She hasn't been home, you see. We don't know — we think she may have . . . run away. And we wondered whether any one of you might know anything about it; if she had perhaps confided in one of you?'

They stared back at her with their lovely transparent eyes, soulless as mermaids'.

Mrs. Merriman ground out hoarsely:

'Try to think — *please* . . . Something . . . *Any* little thing.' She made a queer grimace, and a shadow of alarm crossed their candid faces.

The little girl who had denounced Maureen remarked with a certain brashness: 'She was took off by a bad man, my Mum said.'

Winifred said, in a low voice, 'Don't, Jackie. Don't, dear. Come back with me now. It's just gossip they've picked up; they don't know anything. I promise you it will be all right. It *will* be all right. Come home now. Why, there may be some news waiting for us when we get back. Come, Jackie, come; there's a good girl.'

★   ★   ★

In the café at the crossroads, a woman in an orange apron was stacking dirty cups on a tin tray and wiping a cloth over the tiled tabletops in a yawning desultory way when the man came in with the girl straggling at his heels. Morning Coffees were over, and with irritation the woman saw these fresh customers settle in a corner without speaking. The woman

91

deliberately ignored them, and continued collecting cups and saucers and emptying ashtrays. Once or twice as she moved about she caught sight of them in a mirror; the girl was staring about her vaguely, from time to time splitting her face with enormous yawns, and either scratching her head through her tammy or fingering her thick, unbrushed plaits; the man was leaning on his folded arms, and in the dark corner where they sat, his face could hardly be seen. When at last the woman in the orange apron came across to their table, he said without looking up:

'What can you give us to eat?'

'Oh, we don't do lunches,' said the woman. His face was screened by his hand, but his appearance was unkempt, and she noticed that the little girl's pleated skirt was rumpled, her blazer creased. A queer-looking pair.

'We don't want lunch; just something to eat. Eggs would do. Tea and poached eggs on toast. And some scones, or cakes: whatever you've got.' He glanced up at her briefly.

The woman said sourly, 'I daresay we could manage that. I'll ask the kitchen.'

She could not have said exactly why she felt suspicious of them. Perhaps it was no more than her general loathing of all humanity, with their perverse desire for refreshment at unsuitable hours; or perhaps it was that sixth sense one acquires in the trade which warns one that a customer will try to bilk.

'There's a funny-looking couple just come in, wanting eggs on toast and tea,' she remarked to her friend in the kitchen as soon as the swing door had closed behind her. 'I said I'd ask.'

'What's wrong with them?' Freda asked incuriously, kicking shut the oven door.

'I don't know. They look as though they've been sleeping out all night.'

'Oh, campers.'

'More like tramps, I should say. Probably haven't got a bean. The man's got a sort of look . . . I dunno, I don't trust him.'

'Oh, well, a couple of eggs aren't going to break us. It'll be my Girl Guide good deed for the day. And you can pick the stale scones out of the pig-bin; I daresay they'll be all right when they're heated through. If they're hungry, they won't notice them tasting a bit mouldy!' said she, with a merry laugh.

The tea-room being so empty made Nell speak in a whisper. 'Wasn't she cross-looking?'

'The waitress? I didn't notice.'

'I didn't like her. I didn't like the way she looked at us.'

He said, 'Look, someone's left a paper on the seat over there. Pop across and get it, there's a good lass.'

She hung her head to one side.

'Must I?'

'What's the matter?'

'Suppose she comes back and catches me?'

'Well, she won't eat you, you little juggins.'

With one eye on the service door, holding her breath, Nell darted on tiptoe across the room, snatched up the newspaper with a fiery face, and dashed back clutching it with the desperate intensity of a relay-runner on the final lap. She flung herself back on the chair, puffing and blowing and fanning her hand before her face.

The man ran his eyes over the pages. He folded the paper and began to read a piece about a woman who had been found with her throat cut in a disused air-raid shelter. She had been dead a week, it said.

Suddenly the little girl leaned forward, pointing.

'Oh, look! Do look, George!'

He read on, unhearing. A pulse beat visibly in his rigid jaw. The woman was believed to be a prostitute. It was suspected that robbery was a possible motive for the crime; a handbag with a broken strap, found some distance from the body, contained no money.

'It's me!' cried Nell.

The dead woman was believed to have had about ten pounds on her at the time of her death. The police were anxious to find a man who had been seen with her in a public house, whom they believed could give them some information.

He became aware of the child tugging

his sleeve, and said irritably, 'Well, what is it?'

She whispered excitedly, 'There's a picture of me, look. Do read what it says.' She said again, 'George, do turn over and let's read it,' and, glancing at him anxiously, concerned at his strange silence, saw with surprise that beads of water like tears were trickling down his temples. He seemed not to take in what she was saying, yet he looked frightened.

The paper shook as he turned it over and stared down at the small, smudged print of a child smiling into the sun.

POLICE SEEK MISSING SCHOOL-GIRL, said the headline, and underneath he read:

An intensive search is being carried out by the police for Helen Jennifer Merriman, the nine-year-old school-girl who disappeared from her home four days ago.

The girl is described as slender and approximately 4ft. tall, with blue eyes and fair hair worn in two plaits. When she left home she was wearing her blue school blazer with the monogram E.C.S. in red on the breast pocket, a navy pleated skirt, white blouse, red tam o'shanter, brown shoes and short white socks.

It is believed that she may be in the company of a man with greyish-brown hair, wearing a dark jacket and light grey trousers, who was seen talking with the girl on the afternoon of her disappearance a few hundred yards from her home.

'How do you think they knew — ' Nell began excitedly, but George's quick pressure on her wrist and his warning glance stopped her. He let the paper fall between his knees as the woman in the orange apron approached with her laden tray. In silence, they watched her slamming down the things on the table. In silence, George watched the woman leaving the room, while the little girl put the things in order.

'I should have thought,' he muttered, ravaging a nail. His face was white, glistening like wax. 'Why didn't I realize that your clothes would give you away? That monogram. Of course she noticed it.'

'May I begin, George?' the girl timidly asked. But he didn't answer; his head was turned towards the kitchen entry; and after a moment she surreptitiously picked up a knife and fork and quietly sliced off a neat corner of junkety egg-white and toast.

'That's why she took such a time to bring us the food,' he said. 'They'll have told her to try and keep us here.'

'Your egg's getting cold,' Nell said, licking some yolk from the corner of her mouth.

Suddenly, he pushed away the table. 'We've got to get out of here. Come on.'

'But, George!' she exclaimed in dismay. 'I haven't nearly finished. And you haven't even begun.'

Hastily, he tipped some silver from his purse onto his palm, and laid some coins on the edge of the table.

'Don't argue, there's a good kid. We must hurry. You remarked yourself how she stared.'

Nell, the stupid child, greedily tried to take the remainder of the egg on toast with her. In an attempt to save it from total ruin, she clutched it to her with both hands as it collapsed. She uttered a wail as the yolk dripped thickly from her fingers. Her comical look of disgust only infuriated the man. He had never spoken to her roughly before. Tears came into her eyes at his savage tone. It was her fault that in his haste to get her away he left the newspaper behind.

A bus drew up as they reached the corner, and he pushed her on to it before climbing in after her.

Once upstairs, he said in a low voice, 'Better take off that blazer. You can carry it inside out over your arm. And put your tammy in the pocket.'

'Where are we going, George?'

'Redford.'

'Where's that?'

'A town not far from here. We've got to make fresh plans. The police are looking for us.'

She looked at him, scared.

'Not frightened, are you?'

'Not when I'm with you,' she said.

'You dear little kid, you!' He caught her hand and held it tightly in his. 'You don't know what you mean to me,' he muttered. 'You'll never know how much I love you.' He squeezed her hand hard. 'Stick by me, darling.'

At these words, a deep burning blush suffused her face. Her little feminine soul unfurled within her proudly like a peacock's tail. In a whisper strangled by emotion, she said, 'I love you too. I'll stick by you always.'

★ ★ ★

Freda glanced up at her friend standing in the doorway, and saw at once that something was wrong. She said: 'What's up?'

'They've gone; those two.'

'Without paying?' Freda cried, with pain in her voice.

'No; they've paid,' the other said slowly. 'That's what's so odd. They've eaten none of it. Never even poured out the tea. One

100

of them mauled an egg on toast, that's all.'

'Oh, well!' Freda shrugged. 'So long as they paid, who cares? I've made you a Welsh rarebit. Did you bolt the door?'

'Come and look,' said her friend.

'I don't want to stare at their beastly leavings, dear. I honestly couldn't care less what they ate and what they left.'

'The point is, they didn't eat anything. So what I say is, why did they order it?'

'Perhaps they couldn't wait any longer; had a bus to catch or something. Am I to take your lunch out of the oven or not?'

'I simply want you to come and have a look for yourself, that's all. However much of a hurry they were in, he could have come to the door and asked how much there was to pay, I should have thought, instead of paying a shilling too much. I said there was something funny about them, didn't I?'

'Oh, how you do go on,' said the other in mock complaint, slopping after her into the tearoom in her felt bedroom slippers. 'Well, I honestly can't see what's extraordinary about this.'

'You didn't see them, that's why ... Half the egg on the floor. Ugh!' She bent to scoop it up. 'That was the child, I suppose.'

'You didn't say it was a child. I thought it was a man and woman.'

'A girl, I said.'

'Perhaps she was going to be sick and her father, or her uncle or whoever it was, rushed her out.'

'I suppose he could have come back and at least poured himself a cup of tea afterwards.'

'Oh, go on! I'm going to have my lunch.'

Alone, the woman in the orange apron piled the things back on the tray, straightened the chairs, picked up the newspaper from under the table and, feeling somehow deprived, glanced at it sulkily. She would have cast it down on a chair, but in her moody way it occurred to her to read it while she ate her meal, to punish Freda for not working up an interesting little drama of speculation with her.

Back in the kitchen, she flopped down

on a chair and opened it ostentatiously.

Freda put the plates on the table and sat down facing her friend.

'Don't blame me if it's like boot-leather,' she observed presently. The other took no notice, appeared not to hear. Freda poured out the tea and passed a cup across. She leaned on the table, stirring her tea with a glazed look of boredom on her face, and every few minutes opened her mouth like a hippopotamus in a noisy yawn.

'Poor little mite,' she remarked in an idle conversational manner. 'I wonder what's become of her? It's a marvel to me parents don't go stark out of their minds when things like this happen. I know I should; wouldn't you?'

'Wouldn't I what?'

'Go mad, I was saying.'

'I'm afraid I didn't hear what you were saying.'

'Oh, I'm sorry I interrupted your cogitations; it wasn't important.'

'Well, what was it?'

'It wasn't anything; it doesn't matter.'

'Well, go on, let's have it,' said the

other, putting down the paper with a patient sigh, content now that she had succeeded in annoying her friend.

'It was only a piece in your paper I happened to see, about a schoolgirl who's disappeared — kidnapped by some man, they think. I do think those cases are terrible.'

'I didn't see it.'

'On the other side.'

With an air of indifference, she turned the paper and cast an eye over it as she cut into the Welsh rarebit.

'It's your own fault,' said Freda, observing the long rubbery strands of cheese hanging from her static fork. The fork dropped back on to the plate.

'It's them!' the other woman said in a strange voice. 'I'm perfectly certain of it.' She looked at her friend. 'I told you there was something queer about them.'

'It couldn't be.'

'I'm sure of it. It even describes what they were wearing. You're not going to tell me that's just a coincidence. That explains why they left in such a hurry; he must have seen this — he was

104

reading it, you see — and got the wind up. Oh, my God, fancy that monster being here! It gives me the cold grue to think of it.'

The women gazed at each other with animated, horrified eyes.

Freda said, 'We ought to tell the police.'

'Yes. I'll do it now.'

Freda gave an affected shudder.

'I honestly shan't dare to put my foot outside until he's found.'

'He's probably miles away already. In any case, he's not very likely to come creeping back here to cut *your* throat.'

'Oh, don't!'

'It's people like that wretched prostitute they found in an old air-raid shelter who get their throats cut; they ask for it,' the woman said glibly as she wiped her hands on her orange apron and lifted the receiver.

* * *

Before they left the bus, the man unfastened her plaits and combed the hair loose with his fingers. She wriggled pettishly. 'Why can't I stuff it into my tammy?'

'Because it said in the paper that you were wearing a red tammy.'

'I shall feel silly with it all down round my neck.'

'You don't look silly. You look sweet.'

'It's so babyish,' she grumbled. 'I hate it. I wish I could have it cut off.'

'It's lovely hair,' he said thickly, taking up a handful and softly crunching it together, silky and resilient like some tender living thing. The feel of it excited an extraordinary emotion in him. To think of cutting it off made him tremble. He had positively to drag his hand away from it. He must not think of such things now.

It requires considerable fortitude to go into a town where there seems to be a policeman on every corner, watching for one. The man's hands were slippery with fear. It was only the little girl's candid unconcern, her beautiful trust in him, that enabled him to go through with it.

Crowds were safest, but even among the dense drifting throng of shoppers in Marks & Spencer's he was intensely ill at ease, flinching from the most casual glance. When he had made his purchases, he settled Nell at the snack bar to wait for him till he came back, and told her to order what she liked.

In a back street, he found for a few shillings a pair of old cords and a fisherman's jersey in a filthy junk shop. He didn't dare offer his jacket for sale to the junk merchant, afraid to risk its close inspection, though the stains were almost invisible on the dark stuff. In the Men's public lavatory, he changed his clothes, and then went back to collect the girl.

'What's in there?' asked Nell, prodding the paper carrier as they walked away.

'Things to eat. And some clothes for my pal.'

'For me? What sort of clothes?'

'A blue sweater and some dark red jeans.'

'Jeans! Oh! You are kind! I've wanted jeans all my life, but Mummy would never let me have them.'

'We're going to turn you into a little boy.'

She glanced at him sideways, incredulously, yet ready to believe that nothing was impossible to him, even miracles. 'Really and truly?' she asked. She had always wanted to be a boy, and still had not entirely given up the secret belief that one day it would happen.

He smiled. 'Not really. I shouldn't like you half as much if you were a little boy. We only want other people to think you're one.'

'But I'd like to be one really,' she plaintively said. 'It's rotten being an old girl.'

In that soft voice of his, he said, 'Girls are wonderful.'

'I think they're soppy; I hate them.'

'But if you weren't a girl, you couldn't be my little sweetheart. Girls are something very special. They can do something boys can't do. Only girls can have babies.'

'Silly; mothers have babies, not little girls,' she said scornfully.

He gave his high laugh.

'You darling! What a lovely little kid you are! Mothers are girls to begin with; they only become mothers when they have babies. Did no one ever tell you that? Has no one explained to you about the cave inside you where the babies grow?'

'Of course, I knew it wasn't really the doctor who brought them,' she declared.

'Haven't you ever noticed how big ladies sometimes get in front? That's because they've got a baby inside them.'

She thought about this in silence, while George stroked her hair as they walked, a lovely sleepy sensation. She turned her head and rubbed her cheek against his hand.

'Love me?' he said.

'Mmmm!'

'What a sentimental old couple we are.' They came to a bridge crossing a quiet neglected canal; just the sort of place he'd been watching for.

'Here's a good spot for a foul deed,' he said cheerily. There, on the bank, among the tall grasses and white bells silently ringing on the nettle spires, he made her kneel down. He took out the black-handled knife. He lifted up a handful of the long silky hair. Beneath it the tender small neck showed white as milk, tantalizing him. The knife shook in his hand. *He didn't want to do it.* Sweat was running down his face. Everything had gone dark to his sight except for a piece of bright hair and the white skin beneath it. The blade quivered coldly against the warm flesh, making her shrink, making her cry out. The knife dropped from his grasp.

She screwed round to look at him.

'What are you doing?'

'My hands are shaking.'

'Well, get on with it, you shaky old man, you!'

'I can't,' he said hoarsely, his hands over his face. 'I can't do it.'

'Silly old George, why ever not?'

'I'm afraid,' he said, weeping into his fingers and shuddering.

'Afraid!' she scoffed.

'You can't understand what a man feels. I'm afraid of hurting you.'

'You won't hurt me.'

'You don't know . . . you don't know . . . '

'Oh, goodness, I'm not a baby! I'm not

afraid of your hurting me.'

He caught her to him. 'My little kid,' he muttered huskily. 'My little sweetheart!' He held her to him so tightly that she could feel his body trembling, his heart beating.

★　★　★

It was the merest chance in such a lonely place that the small bundle lying on the bank of the canal should be spotted. It was the scarlet object on top of the heap which attracted the eye of a labourer early the next morning as he cycled past on his way to work. He then recalled vaguely noticing the little pile on his way home the previous evening, and if a random thought had entered his mind concerning it, he could only have concluded that the owner was taking a swim. But to see the bundle still there bothered him. It looked as if there might have been an accident . . . or, worse, someone might have done away with themself. There was no time to leave his bike and cut through the field to have a look for himself. Besides, he didn't want to. It was a job for the police. Perhaps he ought to tell them about it.

Children who go to day school don't have name-tapes in their clothes. The badge on the blazer and the uniform did not correspond to any of the local schools. The policeman examining the blouse for laundry marks, noted regretfully that it had been washed at home. He called to a colleague poking about in the water with a stick.

'Harry! Here a moment! Can you recollect the description of what that schoolkid who disappeared earlier in the week was wearing?'

The other came across to look.

'That's right,' he said. 'E.C.S. Red on navy . . . Think of that! Poor little blighter. Looks as if she's had it.'

The first one said sharply, 'It's a mistake for policemen to jump to conclusions. Before we can say that she's dead, we've got to find the body.'

'Whatever you say, copper,' the one called Harry said resignedly. 'There's nearly four miles of this canal; it's going to be quite a job to fish her out if she's lying somewhere on the bottom in the weeds.'

'We'll come to that later. To begin with, we'll search nearby, starting by beating through the bushes round about. But first you'd better take that lot back to the station and ask the inspector if he can let us have a couple of blokes to lend a hand. Tell him we found the clothes folded tidily on the bank; no sign of a struggle, nothing torn; she evidently removed her clothes herself.'

Harry said sardonically, 'We mustn't take anything for granted though, must we, copper? They might have been taken off her after the poor kid was dead.'

*   *   *

Mrs. Merriman had become almost unrecognizable. Her appearance was frightening. Her chestnut lair lay lank, and as crudely bright against the sunken clay-hued face as hair growing from a skull. From the hollow pits of the eye-sockets two dull pebbles peered, so lifeless that it gave one a shock to see them move. The poor woman could no longer submerge her torment in work about the house. Her fanatical passion for cleanliness had no meaning for her now. Dust lay unobserved. Her eye was no longer irked by chairs left askew, their covers rucked and cushions squashed. Day after day, she dragged on the same crumpled garments, too weary even to comb out her hair. Nothing mattered. She simply waited, in mindless agony.

It was her delusion that if she concentrated the attention of her whole soul unflaggingly on her child, it would keep her alive; held in the circle of her thoughts, no harm could come to her. It was as though her own life was draining out of her in the effort.

Only when Clive came home, haggard and exhausted, did she rouse herself in a brave attempt to prevent him fretting over her. He never knew what it cost her. For it seemed to her that by removing her thoughts from her child even for an instant, she was abandoning her to the terrors she imagined.

When they brought her the little girl's

clothes for identification, the significance at first escaped her. The touchingly familiar little garments sent a flood of joy through her, they seemed to bring Nell so near. Tears washed over the dry stony eyes.

Superintendent Marlowe cleared his throat uncomfortably, mistaking the tears for grief.

'You mustn't give up hope, ma'am. We are still searching.'

Too late, he realized that he had said something terrible.

She said hoarsely:

'I'll never believe it! I know she's alive. If she wasn't, I would know, I would feel it inside me. She is alive.'

To a mother, a child remains forever a part of her living flesh. Even separated by years and distance, she is sensitive in her body to her child's suffering, whether mental or physical. There is no such blind instinct for a father; Merriman had only reason to depend on, and reason is a friendless guide. He understood quite well the degree of hope that existed in the superintendent's mind.

115

Merriman walked down the path to the gate with him where they could be unheard by Jacqueline.

'Just how much chance is there still?' he asked.

Marlowe regarded him in silence gravely.

'They propose to drag the canal tomorrow.'

Merriman's face broke into an odd grimace. Yet after a moment he persisted in a flat voice:

'And if they don't find her . . . '

'We shall go on searching.'

★　★　★

The road traversed a stretch of woodland. A sky of corrugated iron pressed on the tree-tops; soon it would rain. The man in shabby cords and an old fisherman's jersey wandered slowly down the road, a skinny little urchin with a poll of ragged iron-black hair beside him. The startlingly black hair made the blue eyes look very pale in the small white face.

Dead black hair was not so remarkable

116

on the man because it was less of a contrast with his skin and eyes. The illusion of their being taken for father and son was not likely to succeed. The child merely looked queer.

Each time he looked at her, little worms of panic slithered in him queasily. At such moments, it no longer seemed possible to him that they could escape. In the glance of every person who passed, he read suspicion and curiosity. Yet he could not bring himself to abandon the child and seek his safety alone. He depended — his soul depended — utterly on her innocence to protect him, as Catholics confide in the protection awarded by a saint's amulet.

He started, as a cold finger from heaven touched his brow.

'It's raining,' Nell said.

Hand in hand, they ran towards the trees.

The house was there waiting for them. A small brick cottage, windowless, deserted, the exterior licked black by flames. It looked haunted, accursed, a place where some horror had occurred long years ago, a place that people would instinctively avoid: the very place the man needed.

'What a dear little house!' Nell exclaimed. 'Oh, may we just explore?' For one could never be perfectly certain that George would not suddenly turn into one of those impatient adults too intent on their own dull projects to enter into childhood fantasies.

'Rather!' he said. That was what she loved about him. The door grated reluctantly over the stone floor. The walls, leprous, peeling, were draped with crepey black scarves of web that stirred softly in the air. Grass had pushed up between the flags. There was a tiny early Victorian grate in one wall; a flight of slippery broken brick steps in the wall opposite led upwards to the rotten planks above, through which could be seen the rafters in the roof with eyelets of sky winking through. Nell darted through an opening in the third wall to a narrow room beyond with an old stone sink in it, beneath which grew a pretty little cluster of toadstools with weak slimy stems.

'We could make ourselves very snug here,' the man remarked.

'To stay, you mean?'

'We could soon get it looking ship-shape. Clean down the walls with a branch. Light a little fire in the grate; there's plenty of dry wood, at any rate. Nice dry leaves to sleep on. Oh, we could be very cosy. I bet we could live here for years and no one would know.' He laughed excitedly. 'Rent free, too.'

The notion captivated her. Playing 'houses' was always fun, with more immediate charm than the search for a marvellous lost city in the jungles of South America with which he had so long beguiled her (but the sea seemed such a long way off. She sometimes thought they would never get there).

For the man, it was more than a game; it was his last hope. A haven for his desperate need to find a place in which he could hide, scarcely more from his enemies than from himself. His inmost yearning was for a small, dark, safe hole where he could curl up and hide himself from his thoughts. He could feel himself slipping in terror back to that familiar state where, with exhausting vigilance, he had ceaselessly to wrestle to maintain his hold on his mind as if it was a thing separate from himself. The derelict, bird-haunted cottage offered at least the security of concealment. A place where he could be alone with the uncorrupted innocence and affection he craved, far from the evil of the world by which he was pursued. He buried himself desperately in the present, not looking beyond the time when their meagre supplies of food and money should run out, because beyond that there was nothing to envisage — nothing but the last escape of all.

For a day or two, the protection of four walls allowed him a blessed sense of safety. And then one evening, as they lay before the smoky flickering fire, watching the stars like pins glinting between the branches, and talking philosophically of life, and God, and the destiny of men and animals, he was seized by anxiety; like a premonition. He caught her to him.

'What should I do if I lost you?' he groaned.

'But, George,' she expostulated, 'I couldn't get lost, I never go far enough away.'

'One day they'll find us. Yes, it's inevitable; I see it now.'

'Why need they? You said they never would here,' she exclaimed, his agitation communicating itself to her.

'That is how it will end.' He shivered with anguish. 'They will tear you away from me. I shall never see you again.'

'Oh, no, George! No! Don't let them find us! I don't want never to see you again. If we explain to them — '

'They'll tell you why. They'll tell you I'm a very wicked man and must be taken away and punished — '

'No! No!' she cried.

'I won't tell you what they do to men who steal little girls.'

'You didn't steal me! I'll tell them you didn't!' She broke into tears. 'I *want* to stay with you for ever. I love you.' A passion of hysteria rose in her, augmented by the night rustling round them and his heart beating thickly against her.

He rocked her gently back and forth, as

people rock in grief or pain. There were tears in his eyes.

'How can I let you go? How could I bear it?' he said huskily. 'You're all I have. All I've ever known of love and tenderness. You're part of my very self — the best part. You're my own lost innocence. If I lost you, I should be lost indeed. I wouldn't want to live.' She saw his eyes glinting with tears in the firelight as he turned his head. 'I'd rather kill myself. I'd rather kill myself now.'

'Oh, don't, George, please. Don't say that,' she wailed, pressing her arms around him. 'You mustn't. I don't want to be left all alone. I'd be so scared.' She could feel him trembling in her frantic embrace.

He whispered eagerly, 'But I wouldn't leave you alone, my darling. You could come with me, if you wanted to. Then we'd always be together, just as we are now; no one could ever take you away from me; and nothing, nothing, would ever spoil you; you'd always be the same perfect, precious, little unspoilt girl.'

Infected by his excitement without in

the least understanding what he meant, she said weeping, 'I want to go with you wherever you go.'

'You wouldn't be afraid?' he tenderly murmured, hugging her close.

She drew a long quivering breath and licked away the tears with her tongue.

'I'm never afraid when I'm with you, George.'

'Ahhh!' he cried softly on a note between anguish and ecstasy. '*Faithful little heart!*' He put a hand to her breast where its small rapid tick could be felt. '*Faithful unto death!*'

★ ★ ★

Smoke from the ruined cottage was observed floating lazily above the trees. It was not long before the attention of the local police was drawn to it by the rumour of a man and a child lurking in the vicinity. A little quiet investigation was called for. Nothing that could alarm them, if they should turn out to be the wanted pair.

A chap in dungarees drifted idly along

the road, seated himself on a log not far from the deserted cottage, and opened a pack of sandwiches. Presently he saw a man in fawn cords and an old jersey come out of the house and go towards the stream with a couple of cans, and after a moment the workman in dungarees strolled across to the cottage and leaned against the window's empty frame. The child kneeling on the floor, absorbed in feeding sticks into the fire, looked up as the window darkened.

'Hullo!' the man said amiably. 'What are you up to?'

'Nothing,' said the child.

'And what might your name be?'

'Ned,' the child said, with a cold look.

'Get on!' said the man, astonished. 'I took you for a little girl.'

'I'm a boy,' the child said shortly, bending its head to hide the flush that swept over the pale dirty face.

'Wasn't half surprised to see you in there,' the man went on in a casual tone. 'Didn't know anyone lived here.'

The child made no reply, poking a stick carefully into the cage of twigs.

'You here all alone?' said the man in his hatefully friendly voice.

'No, I'm not,' said the child, casting him a quick suspicious glance, and adding like a threat: 'I'm with my father and he'll be back in a minute.'

'Camping, are you? I've done a bit of camping in my time too. Mostly up on the Ring. That's a good place. Know it?'

'No.'

'Ah, then you don't come from these parts. Everyone round here knows the Ring.'

The child busily broke up the remaining sticks into pieces no larger than splinters, for the sake of appearing too intent to answer.

'Well,' said the man at last, 'I must be getting along,' and off he drifted.

Later that afternoon, a large dark-blue car drew up a couple of hundred yards down the road, and five men descended and began walking in silence towards the burnt-out cottage. Two of the men suddenly broke away and turned into the wood.

He became aware of her frantic fingers tugging him awake.

'George! Oh, please! They're coming here. I'm sure they are. Three policemen. Oh, what shall we do?'

That they had come for him at last was his first conscious thought, to be succeeded by a hideous confusion of ideas like a vertigo of the mind. With a face as white as stone, he scrambled up and ran for the slippery crumbling steps leading to the broken floor above: a place to hide from them for a moment longer. And, halfway up, paused giddily, appalled to realize that his panic had nearly driven him into a trap.

'Oh, quick, George, quick,' the girl whimpered, wringing her hands. 'They're nearly here.'

With the demented courage of a baited animal he darted to the window, holding the girl to him with quivering hands. He saw the three men stepping across the grass verge. Their terrible impassive faces stared back at him. The Voice that came to him in moments of extreme peril, that directed him when he was beyond himself, was repeating over and over, 'Be not afraid of their faces . . . Be not afraid of their faces . . . '

He called to them hoarsely: 'What do you want?'

'Just a word with you, I think,' said the one in the peaked cap.

The Voice said, 'Remember, you've got the girl!' His hand fumbled for and found the black knife with its unanswerable potency.

He screamed at them to keep back. They saw the light flash off the steel as he raised it in the air, and brought it down to within an inch of the child's throat. The child's eyes, ringed with terror, stared out of her paper-white face.

The first man halted and lifted his arms in a gesture that brought his companions to a standstill. They were some fifteen yards yet from the house. Hopeless at that distance to attempt to rush him. The child would be dead before they got inside the door.

The man in the peaked cap said in a steady voice, 'All right. You win. We won't come any nearer. But put away that knife, there's a good chap; you're frightening the little girl.'

'It's you she's afraid of, not me,' the man insanely declared. He looked desperate, crazy, terrified. 'If you try to take us, I shall kill her and then myself.'

In one part of his mind the man in the peaked cap was trying to calculate how much time there was still to get through. He would have liked to glance at his watch, except that he dared not let his gaze flicker, dared not for an instant cease to hold the man's wild eyes with his own.

'Steady on,' he said. 'Don't lose your head. There's no need to do anything foolish. We're not going to touch you.' He shifted one foot slightly till it came to rest against a stone.

The lunatic said, in a high, hysterical voice:

'I'll give you just thirty seconds to clear off. She'll come to no harm if you leave us alone. This isn't a threat, it's a warning.'

'Look here,' said the other in a reasonable tone, 'what are you getting so fussed about? It's not you we're after.

Send the girl out to us and we'll not bother you further.'

'Ten seconds!' cried the man, his eyes wide and blind with terror. 'I'm going to do it!' he screamed.

'Don't be a fool!' shouted the policeman, keeping his hands to his sides but his whole body leaning forward as if despite himself it was going to rush forwards. He saw the light run along the blade in a flickering movement. He exclaimed with desperate urgency:

'Wait a minute! Here's something you haven't thought of . . . ' Using any words to hold the man's attention a moment longer, without any idea of what he would say next, his only thought was to keep him talking.

He saw the man at the window turn his head for a fraction of an instant, as though distracted by a sound behind him. It was the moment the policeman had been waiting for. In one swift smooth movement he bent, picked up the stone at his foot, and hurled it straight at the man's face, catching him between the eyes. The three men ran forward.

Then everything happened at once. Too fast for Nell to comprehend. She heard George scream as he reeled away from her. And saw him seized by two other policemen who were suddenly there in the room behind them. The room was crowded with policemen. And something terrible was happening, a silent struggle going on with no sound but their heavy breathing and their boots grating and slipping on the stone floor. Their huge thick bodies came between her and her last appalling glimpse of George writhing among them like something inhuman, his face no face at all but a mass of shiny red paint out of which glared two quite expressionless eyes. She began to shriek, her heart filled with an insupportable terror. And then an immense hand was clapped across her eyes and she was lifted and whirled away.

She was bumped in someone's arms as they ran with her down the road. 'It's all over, kiddy; it's all right. You're safe now. It's all over,' he was saying, as he sat with her in the back of the police car, holding her in his arms. The buttons of his jacket hurt her cheek.

'I want George,' she sobbed. 'I want George.'

'Yes, yes,' he said reassuringly, 'George is coming. He'll be here presently,' supposing she was crying for her brother, or perhaps a dog — you never knew with kiddies. Even if it had occurred to him that 'George' might be the name by which she knew Leonard Wheedler, he would not have conceived it possible that it could be for this terrifying maniac that her small frame was shaken with such desolate sobs.

★ ★ ★

She sat on a hard chair by the police station fire with a mug of tea in one hand and a doorstep of bread and butter in the other. The bread turned and turned in her mouth and would not be swallowed; fear had dried up her mouth. She washed it down with a gulp of the scalding sweet tea and furtively laid the rest of the slice on the edge of her chair. It had come to her in this last hour that her parents were going to be very, very angry with her. She comprehended only now that she had done something abominable in running away, and suddenly she was terrified of seeing them again, of some unimaginable punishment that would be inflicted on her for a naughtiness that was unheard of in the children's calendar of crimes.

A policeman came in and said cheerfully, 'Your mummy and daddy have arrived.'

It scarcely seemed possible that the child could turn any paler. She stood up and ran a tongue across her lips.

The moment of confronting was terrible for all three. If the child had run to them gladly, it would have been easy; the tears of joy that kept spilling from the mother's eyes would have poured freely down, and the child would have been caught into her arms and held close, close . . .

That was how Mrs. Merriman had imagined it would be. But at sight of the child, as she and her husband entered the room, they were transfixed. For one horrified moment they thought there had been a mistake. Their glances flashed towards one another in dismay: *this* wasn't, couldn't be, Nell. And the child's pale frozen eyes stared back at them expressionlessly, no recognition illuming the pinched white face. What connection could there be between this starveling with a head of rough black feathers and their sparkling little girl with her long blonde hair? What had happened to her? God, what had happened to her to make her look like that? A lump rose up into the mother's throat, choking her.

It was an anguish of embarrassment to be observed by strangers at such a moment. The policemen stood around watching the little scene with pleased innocent grins. It was impossible to be natural in their presence. They stood there stiffly, not knowing how to negotiate the gulf.

With an effort, Mrs. Merriman brought a smile of some sort to her lips, unable to speak for the pain in her throat, and at the same time Mr. Merriman said in a husky voice: 'Hullo, Nell.'

The child opened her mouth, but no sound came. Her mouth was so dry that she had to put up a finger to release her tongue before she could croak out, 'Hullo, Daddy.'

It was better once they were in the car and driving away. Mrs. Merriman lifted the child onto her lap. The shivering little body was rigid and unyielding in her arms. There was nothing of her, a mere bag of bones encased in cold trembling flesh. The mother's tears fell on to the child's face.

'My baby!' she wept. 'My precious baby! I've got you back!'

Perhaps they were not going to be so dreadfully angry with her, after all. The child's resistance suddenly collapsed. She subsided against her mother and dissolved into tumultuous tears. '*Oh, Mummy!*'

'There, there, darling. Don't cry. Mummy's got you. You're all right now, baby. You're all right now.'

'I'm so frightened!'

'It's all right, baby. Mummy's got you.'

'What did they do to George, those

policemen? What's going to happen to him?'

'They've taken him away, darling. He'll never find you again, I promise. They'll shut him away and lock him up so that he can never get out any more. It's all over now. It was just a bad dream. Don't think about it. There's nothing to be afraid of any more. Mummy's got you safe.'

Nell said, on an in-caught breath, 'I didn't like what they were doing to him.'

'Don't think about it, my precious.'

She pressed her eyes into her mother's neck.

'His face was all bloody.'

'Try not to think about it, darling. You shall sleep with Mummy tonight, in case you feel frightened. We'll make Daddy sleep in your bed, shall we?'

'He said something dreadful would happen to him if they caught him.' She raised her tear-blurred eyes to peer at her mother's face. 'Why, Mummy?'

'You see, he was a very wicked man, darling.'

She cried out passionately: 'He wasn't wicked! He was good. The goodest man

I've ever met. I loved him. We were so happy together. He said I was his little sweetheart,' she said tearfully, trying to defend, to explain, to excuse the inexcusable, the indefensible, the inexplicable.

Mrs. Merriman went cold to the roots of her hair with the shock.

'You can't know what you're saying. How can you talk of loving someone who took you away from your mummy and daddy?'

'He didn't take me. He *said* that was what everyone would say. He said they'd all say he'd stolen me, and that was why he would have to be punished. He didn't steal me. I wanted to go with him. I asked to go. He didn't steal me, Mummy. Tell them he didn't. Please, Mummy,' she wept.

'He's made you believe that was how it happened; but it can't have been like that,' her mother protested in an unfamiliar voice. 'No little girl could want to run away with a strange man, she'd be too afraid. And only someone very wicked and cruel would have taken her if she did.'

'I went with him because he loved me. He needed me,' the child declared. 'He told me so.'

Mrs. Merriman wet her parched lips.

'What do you mean, dear: he needed you? What did he need you for?' Her voice trembled.

'He needed me to live with him. We were going to find a lost city in the jungle. He said he couldn't live without me. He said if they came and took me away, he'd kill himself. I'm so afraid!' she sobbed. 'Make them let him come back, Mummy! I want him to come back!'

Fear gripped the mother's heart in icy fingers. A black wave of nausea rose up and engulfed her. She cried out to God who had saved her child. She cried out that He to whom all things were possible should make the impossible, impossible. In a voice that she tried hard to keep steady, she said, 'I don't quite understand, dear. What do you mean by 'living' with him?'

'We wanted to live together, for ever, like grown-up people.'

'I don't . . . I can't . . . ' she muttered.

'I mean, he didn't ever do anything to you, did he, that he — he shouldn't have done?' Mrs. Merriman said desperately.

'He didn't want to, honestly, Mummy. But he had to.'

'Tell Mummy,' she said in a faint voice, 'what he did to you.'

The girl said in surprise, 'He cut off my hair. He hated doing it. It was to make me look like a boy, you see. It'll soon grow again, Mummy, and all this black will come out when you wash it.'

'He did nothing else? Nothing *wrong*?'

'Only once,' the little girl said in a small ashamed voice, remembering the eggs George had stolen for their breakfast. She should never have admitted it, she thought, her heart beating with fear for him; now perhaps they would send him to prison. She would say no more, tell nothing.

The darkening landscape flowed steadily past. 'Try and tell Mummy about it?' Mrs. Merriman muttered huskily.

But the little girl was afraid. She didn't answer.

The mother tried again.

'Tell me what happened, darling? Mummy won't be cross with you. What did he do?'

Unreasoning panic rose in the child's mind. Blindly seeking to defend George, she quavered, 'I don't want to tell you. I don't want to talk about it.'

Incomprehension and terror grew in them both with every question, with every answer. Their minds, running along different lines, could no longer meet at a point of understanding.

★ ★ ★

Nell never did comprehend what it was that was so terribly 'wrong' about the episode. She only knew it must be something ugly because it was unmentionable. It frightened her to see their faces freeze when she asked about him. It left her with a feeling of guilt and shame. She learnt never to speak of him, never to mention George's name. He had been bad in some way they couldn't explain to her. It was something she had best forget.

The interlude — enclosed and perfect in its bright happy colours as a tiny scene in a *camera obscura* — was darkened by a sense of sin; became dreamlike . . . vague . . . and at last faded from her memory altogether.

Yet something was lost. Something for which she would search for the rest of her life, without knowing it, and never find again.

Death of an Artist

Murder a man for a yard of canvas! It sounds cold-blooded to the point of insanity, doesn't it? Yet that was what Adrian Manley, that kind, peaceable man, proposed to do.

Adrian was a painter, though you have never heard of him — unless perhaps you move in Bohemian circles, and even then . . . He wasn't of any importance, you see, although he had devoted his whole life to his art. Somehow he lacked the divine spark. He never acknowledged that lack, maintaining stoutly that one day the world would recognise him. In spite of that, he lacked no skill in execution, he had great technical ability. What money he had was earned by copying famous paintings for the dealers. Maybe too much copying had spoiled any style he might have had. But what did it matter? He painted, he earned money enough to provide bread and wine, he had an adorable little wife, and he was really awfully happy — until Simon Short came along.

The gods had given a lot to Simon Short. Besides good looks and an attractive personality, they had bestowed the gift of genius. Or so people said. Whether that brilliant, rather flamboyant, painting would outlast his life in value was another matter. He had his glory now, and that was all that mattered to him. Fame, admiration, riches, women at his feet adoring him. So that Adrian felt it was a little unfair that Simon should have chosen *his* wife to run away with, when there were so many lovely women only too willing to leave their husbands for Simon. Adrian had been very cut up about that, and soon after their elopement to Spain he had left London and settled in a small fishing village in Cornwall. Time made him less lonely.

And then Simon came back to England. Presumably it was coincidence, because Simon was not really foolhardly, that made him choose to settle in Adrian's village.

When Adrian ran into Simon at the tobacconist's, his large red face went pale and shiny with sudden sweat. But Simon was in no way embarrassed and greeted him joyously.

'You *must* come in and see us, old chap.' he insisted, his white teeth gleaming charm in the dim shop. 'Lucy would simply love to see you.'

So Lucy was with him. He massaged the green corduroy of his trouser-leg with a sandalled foot as he tried to conjure from his confused mind some reason for not visiting them.

But Simon took his acquiescence for granted. So that was that. He stood there in the narrow, sunlit street, slim and broad-shouldered, consciously handsome with his dark-tanned face contrasting with his sun-bleached hair, laughing kindly at funny old Adrian as he shambled away. How could Lucy ever have married such a creature? Just like a huge, red bear, only flabbier. So ugly, so clumsy, so very uninteresting. Well, women were incomprehensible, he decided platitudinously.

Adrian spent the evening there and was relieved and somewhat hurt to find that Lucy was unchanged, quite well and quite happy. She seemed genuinely glad to see him and talked nostalgically of the old days.

Simon said, 'That's an awfully pretty girl in the baker's shop, Adrian. I've asked her to pose for me. That always fetches 'em.' He laughed boyishly and winked.

Lucy looked at him from under her full white lids; and Adrian knew that she had no illusions about Simon's constancy. He wondered if the knowledge hurt her, if it had been hard to come by. The thought made him tug fiercely at his coarse red moustache.

Even that would have passed over all right if Simon hadn't condescended to show off his latest work to his guest. Adrian was enough of an artist to submerge jealousy in artistic appreciation.

'And this,' said Simon, 'is my masterpiece; at least, I think so. Tell me what you think of it, old boy. No one is more qualified to judge than you whether I have caught her personality. Anyway, it's a fine bit of painting, if I do say it myself, and I'm going to exhibit it at the Academy next year.' And he produced his *piece de resistance*.

It was a portrait of Lucy sewing. Her pale face glowed transparently above the dark green of her patterned frock, a vase of gaudy tulips stood at her elbow on a yellow wooden table, the background was richly striped in deep rose and lilac. And in the midst of this brilliance of colour and composition sat Lucy, sewing. Her full white lids covered her eyes, the dark lashes lay softly on her pale cheeks, her lips curved upward in a hinted smile, subtle shadows played round her temples under the shadow of her shining hair; her long, boneless, sensuous, Italianate hands held the white stuff she was sewing with a time-aged gesture. Yes, it was Lucy — the real Lucy!

The sudden flood of bitterness threatened to overwhelm Adrian in its intensity. It was then that he first felt the violence of this urge to kill Simon — to smash, destroy, annihilate this man who had taken so much from him. *He* should have been the one to paint that picture of Lucy, the picture that would have brought him fame, the picture that was executed by a genius. He had never had a chance to paint Lucy like that, too busy pot-boiling to earn money for her . . . and then they said he was nothing but a copyist. It wasn't fair, it wasn't fair.

As soon as he could, Adrian crept away. That night, he had terrifying, tormented dreams, from which he woke screaming, his eyes starting from his head with fear. But he knew then he was going to kill Simon if ever he had the opportunity — he wouldn't be able to help himself. He spent the rest of the night wrapped in an old overcoat that served as a dressing-gown, sitting in his one armchair in his dark studio, staring out of the window at the ghostly moonlit garden . . . planning

Obviously, he decided, it must look like an accident. A push over the edge of a cliff, for instance. Only then there was the danger of being seen. No, somehow he must provide an alibi. The whole thing would need very careful planning and much thought, because he didn't intend to be caught and hanged for ridding the world of a swine like that. He could take his time over the affair; there was no hurry, no need to get flustered and make some irremediable error simply through lack of time and forethought. No, he would make no mistake. This would be a perfect crime. A masterpiece of a crime. Yes. Adrian, the copyist and pot-boiler, would create a masterpiece for the first time in his life. And so the central detail of his plot was born.

He felt an unaccustomed well-being and self-confidence these days. A triumphant sense of power at the thought that soon Simon would exist no longer, he would just cease to be — and that gift of death lay in Adrian's hands. It made him feel like God.

Gradually, piece by piece, like a jigsaw puzzle, his plan matured. Soon it was all ready, and with pride he waited for a propitious day — a day when Lucy would be safely out of the way. And when that day came he was ready.

Lucy had gone to London for the

weekend, ostensibly to visit her parents — but, in fact, as Adrian and many of the villagers realised, to leave the field free for the play of Simon's brief passion for the baker's daughter. *Therefore, I must set to work — and quickly*, thought Adrian, his face suffused with scarlet by the fiery racing of his pulse.

Simon was kneeling on the floor of his studio stretching a canvas when Adrian arrived. He brandished a hammer cheerfully, smiling as well as he was able around the nails he held in his mouth.

'Let me help you,' said Adrian, kneeling at his side.

Together they tugged evenly at the canvas, hammering the nails neatly along the edges until the material was smoothly stretched over its wooden frame.

'I'm glad you liked that portrait of Lucy,' Simon said.

'Yes. I wish you'd let me buy it from you.'

Simon laughed. 'Come, come, my dear fellow, that's sheer sentimentality. You wouldn't want to buy it if it wasn't Lucy. Own up, now. Besides, I expect to get a thousand quid for it after the exhibition, so it's hardly likely I'd sell it to you for twenty or thirty, is it?'

Adrian rose to his feet and walked across to the window. It was hard to control his mounting fury; difficult to suppress the impulse to cry out that it was *his* picture, that Simon had stolen the idea from him, as he had stolen so much else. But Simon was talking about the baker's daughter; eulogising her gleaming, honey-coloured skin, her sulky, sensuous mouth, praising her supple body and strong, sturdy limbs.

Adrian interrupted him, his face oddly white against the scarlet of his hair. 'You're a dirty swine, Simon, aren't you? You can't keep your hands off anything in skirts, can you?'

'It's the artistic temperament, old boy. Besides, they simply can't resist me, you know,' he said, with a charming smile.

'Yes, *you* can have anyone you want. You didn't need to take Lucy from me — '

'You surely don't bear me a grudge, after all this time?' His astonishment was real. 'But, my dear chap, just think of the disillusionment you've been spared. You ought to be grateful to me. Believe me, Lucy isn't all — '

'For God's sake, shut your mouth,' Adrian spat at him, and his hand tightened on the hammer he still held.

Simon stared at him for a moment or two. 'Sorry, old chap. I didn't know you felt like that about her,' he said at last.

The fool! Of course he didn't feel 'like that' about her. That was only memory. It was the picture — that glorious piece of painting — that was making him choke and burn with jealousy, a jealousy that no woman could rouse in his breast. He mustn't lose his temper, though, or he might do something foolish. *Be cautious; wait for the most advantageous moment*, he told himself.

Aloud, he said, 'Let's drop the subject, Simon. As a matter of fact, I only dropped in to borrow a canvas off you. I've run short and I don't want to go in to Amchester today. You don't mind, do you?'

'Of course not. Come on up and

choose what you like.'

They mounted the narrow stairway that led to the small gallery where Simon kept his unused stock. Adrian chose one carelessly; his heart was thumping so heavily in his throat that he could scarcely breathe. When Simon turned to descend the stairs, Adrian was close behind him, his eyes focusing on a little patch of the sun-bleached hair low down close behind his ear.

The hammer descended on that little patch of hair at the same instant that Adrian stuck his foot in front of Simon's ankle as he moved to the first step. With a sickening rush, Simon hurtled past the ladder-like stairs, thudded to a hideous huddle below, and lay still . . .

Adrian leaned against the wall, fighting the threatening blackness; his red hair was dark with sweat and his lungs heaved spasmodically. Somewhere in his head, a pulse drummed: *Done, done, done done.* With an effort, he pulled himself together; there was still a lot to be done — and in a very short space of time. The thought of what still lay before him seemed to revive and inspire him with fresh courage. Boldly now, he walked down the stairs and examined the crumpled form at the bottom. Yes, he was dead. A pity that he had not fallen on the back of his head; that would have excused that faint discolouration behind the ear. Too dangerous to move him over, though; might not arrange him in a possible way. Better to leave things as they were. Even if that bruise was noticed, even if they suspected foul play, they would never think of him — he would have a perfect alibi.

He pulled out a handkerchief, carefully wiped the hammer all over, forced the dead man's limp hand round it; and then, carrying it by its handkerchief-wrapped tip, deposited it among the nails that lay beside the freshly stretched canvas.

Next, still using the handkerchief, he pulled from under the dead man's outflung arm the canvas he had so recently chosen and set it on the easel. The palette had already been prepared by Simon for the still-life arrangement which was stood on a table in the room: bright blossom in a Chinese vase on a blue-and-yellow patterned cloth. It was a lovely composition, and the colours were as gay as a summer noon.

Adrian felt the excitement rising in him. Now for his alibi. Here was the crucial point of his planned masterpiece. He was a copyist, was he? Well, he was going to show the world just what a brilliant copyist he was. This picture was going to be painted in Simon Short's inimitable style, and no one would ever know the difference. Fortunately, Simon worked mainly with a palette-knife, for the paint stayed wet longer that way — and Adrian wanted the paint to stay wet as long as possible. No one was likely to call at the studio during the day — except, perhaps the baker's daughter, and Adrian was going to fix that all right. Therefore Simon should not be found till nightfall, and then it would appear that he had been working all day on the painting — and that, as dusk fell, maybe he had gone to the gallery to get something, and on his way down had missed his footing in the half-light.

And very nice too, thought Adrian, triumphant. He seized the palette-knife and began work. Cautiously at first, but more and more frenziedly as he progressed and inspiration flowed freely. With strong slashing strokes he transferred the riot of colour before him to the canvas.

Ah, this was real painting! The headiness of using fresh, flamboyant colour after the sombre and delicate tints necessary in copying Old Masters! Extravagantly, he splashed on great gouts of pure, flaming colour, and smoothed it into swirling patterns with his fingertips. But never for an instant did he forget what he was doing — that he was painting the picture that Simon would have painted that day . . . if he had still been alive. And when at last it was finished and he stepped back from the easel, he saw that it was good. The juxtaposition of colours, the very way the knife strokes lay one beside the other, the brilliance and verve of execution, all seemed to shout Simon's signature. Adrian was more than satisfied.

Carefully, he wiped the palette-knife clean of fingerprints and thrust it into Simon's loosely clenched right fist. Sharply, he glanced about the studio — was there anything he had overlooked? — no, everything was realistically in order. There was no trace anywhere of an intruder. One last admiring glance at the painting with the well-known sprawling red signature in the right-hand corner — *Simon Short* — and he had left the studio with its strangely still tenant behind him.

Outside in the sharpness of the morning air, he was glad to see that the sun had not yet climbed halfway up the sky. He had worked fast. The greater part of the day lay still before him. And now to confirm his alibi.

He strolled leisurely down the village street and entered the baker's shop. The scent of freshly baked bread struck him in a warm wave. Suddenly he felt ravenously hungry. *Nothing like a spot of fast-moving crime to give you an appetite*, he giggled inwardly.

He leant across the counter. 'Hello,

Miriam.' he said amiably. 'Would you give a hot, indigestible roll and a glass of milk to a starving man?'

The Cornish girl smiled. 'Father's just brought in the milk, Mr. Manley, and the new bread is in the basket at your elbow.'

Adrian crammed half a roll into his capacious mouth. ''S'good. I've just been over to Mr. Short's,' he volunteered conversationally.

'I'm going over there myself soon. He wants me to sit for my portrait,' she said proudly.

'I know. He told me. Matter of fact, that's why I came over now; he gave me a message for you. He's very busy, working on a new idea, and he wondered if you'd mind very much postponing the sitting till later. He wondered whether you could go over there this evening instead.'

The bright blue eyes clouded with disappointment. 'Not much point in me going there when it's dark, is there? He can't paint me at night.'

Adrian smiled wryly. Was she playing the innocent, or was she truly only interested in the glory of posing for a *real*

158

artist? 'Possibly he wants to paint you by artificial light,' he suggested. 'In any case, he doesn't want you today; he's too preoccupied and, as usual when he's working hard, he's in a foul temper. I just went over to borrow a canvas and he nearly bit my head off for interrupting him.' Adrian laughed shortly.

'Well, I don't know that Dad'll let me go at night,' the girl said dubiously. 'That Mr. Short, he's ever so nice, and — oh, I don't know, sometimes he gets funny — I like him — and I like his wife, too — only sometimes he gets funny. Seems like artists is queer,' she summed up.

He chuckled at her sudden embarrassment. 'Never mind, Miriam.' He patted her plump hand. 'He won't do you any harm, I promise you. He's quite harmless. Heavens, I must be off! I want to catch the 11.15 to Amchester.' He swallowed the milk at a draught, plonked down a coin, and strode from the shop.

He strolled about the little market town of Amchester, a noticeably bizarre figure. Shapeless, paint-stained, green corduroy suit; magenta, open-necked sports shirt pulled tightly across his barrel chest, and ornamented with a cadmium yellow tie; no hat upon his coarse, unbrushed, flaming hair; and, to complete the vision, a streak of cobalt across one fat cheek, and a length of bast tied round his apology for a waist to keep his braceless trousers from disaster. But he didn't care. The more people turned to stare, the better pleased he was; since, after all, a man cannot be in two places at once.

He didn't go to a pub for his lunch; he went instead to the most respectable café he could find, although his stomach grumbled at the fancy trifles he was offered. Afterwards, he sat on the primitive promenade until the collector dawdled along to give him a ticket for the hire of the deckchair, in exchange for tuppence proffered by Adrian. The ticket was valid for two hours only, and was stamped with the date and hour. Adrian placed it in his pocket. He sighed contentedly, lay back in the deckchair, and dropped into a light doze. Presently, he awoke with a shiver; the sky was overcast, and it looked like rain. A little further along the front stood the Amchester Picture Palace de Luxe, and towards this Adrian hurried just as the first drops spattered on the pavement. He leant back in the stuffy twilight and stared unseeingly at the elephantine figures on the screen.

It was hard to realise that Simon was dead; harder still to realise that he had killed him. Now he would be able to get hold of that portrait of Lucy, too. Lucy would sell or give it to him — she would never realise its importance. And he could keep it or destroy it, just as he felt inclined. Was it morally wicked, he wondered, to destroy a work of art? He decided that, however much he wanted to, he would never be able to tear up the picture; that was too much against his principles. Art first and last with him. And yet, he thought indignantly, people said he was not a real artist, merely a copyist. He'd show 'em. And all those people would see now whether their idol's work stood the test of time. Bah! The adulated fool! He had only ever produced one *real* thing, and that was shortly going to be safely in Adrian's custody.

He glanced at the faintly illuminated clock above the exit. Nearly time to go. He had some odds and ends of shopping to do, and then he would catch the evening bus back to the village.

He arrived back shortly before nine o'clock, just after the body had been discovered. Miriam had gone to the studio that evening, and been surprised to find the place still and dark, since the slow spring dusk had been descending for some time. She had been more amazed still to find the door open and to receive no answer to her call. Timidly, she had gone in, found and lit a lamp, and — and then she had seen it . . . Lying there so horribly still and tense . . . And then scream after scream had torn shrilly, terrifyingly, through the peaceful air . . .

The police worked hard throughout the night, but it was not till the next day that they began their routine questioning. As a friend of the deceased and one of the last people to have seen him alive, Adrian went to the police station to give what help he could.

Detective Inspector Rutherford looked up from the pile of papers on the desk before him. 'Nice of you to have come round so promptly,' he said cordially. 'I wanted to see you badly. You seem to have been the last person to have seen the deceased alive. Now, what time would that have been?'

Adrian pursed his mouth like a pouting baby. 'About ten in the morning, I should think. I wasn't really paying much attention, you know.'

'Quite. And did he seem in good spirits? Not depressed or worried about anything?'

Adrian shook his head. 'Not that I noticed. But he wouldn't have confided in me, anyway. No, he seemed all right.'

'Sure? I had the impression that you mentioned to someone that he was bad-tempered — 'in a foul temper', to use your own words.'

'Oh, that! That was just because he was working, and was irritated at being interrupted. He was always like that; most of us are,' he said with a little laugh.

'Yes. I'm sorry to be such a nuisance.

163

These routine questions . . . ' He waved a hand, as if dismissing a bothersome fly. 'One's duty, and so on. However, just why did you — er — interrupt him?'

'I'd run out of canvas, so I went to borrow some from him.'

Rutherford was curt. 'Yet Miss Miriam Trelawney affirms that when you entered the baker's shop — which, according to your statement, you went to straight from Mr. Short's studio — you were empty-handed.'

The unobtrusive constable in the corner looked up from his writing. Adrian suppressed a contemptuous smile. 'Because I didn't take a canvas from him after all. As I said, he was annoyed at being disturbed at the inception of his work, so I left him to it. I decided to go to Amchester, instead, as there were other things I needed as well.'

'But in spite of his annoyance, he gave you a message to be delivered immediately to Miss Trelawney, cancelling the arrangements he had made with her the day before.'

He nodded.

'He was going to paint her, wasn't he? Didn't it strike you as odd that he chose, quite suddenly, to paint something else?'

'Not in the least,' said Adrian coldly. 'And I'm afraid that I don't understand what you're driving at, Inspector. What has all this to do with the death of Mr. Short?'

Rutherford seemed to hesitate for a moment. 'I haven't been quite open with you, Mr. Manley,' he said at last. 'Mr. Short did not meet with an accident — he was murdered.'

The painter sucked in his fat cheeks in amazement. 'Murdered,' he echoed faintly. 'What makes you think so? Why should anyone want to murder Simon? Who did it?'

Constable and Detective Inspector watched him in silence. At length, Rutherford, ignoring his questions, said, 'So I am sure you will want to help us as much as you can in tracking down the perpetrator.'

Adrian bowed his head. To his relief, the detective now began talking about

Amchester, and he produced a detailed account of his day there. He showed him the chair ticket, the cinema, the bills for his various purchases.

Rutherford smiled at the slips of paper lying meekly as mute evidence on the desk. 'Do you always carry about useless bits of paper? Your pockets must be filled with rubbish.'

'They are. I'm frightfully absent-minded; the artistic temperament, I suppose.' He laughed easily. But inwardly, he wasn't laughing, he was rattled. The pit of his stomach was contracting nervously and the palms of his hands were damp. It was absurd to think that they could possibly have anything against him, and yet there was a subtle undertone to these questions that was — menacing. He had made no mistake, he knew that. They were probably thoroughly bewildered as to the whys and wherefores of Simon's death, and were merely making angry stabs in the dark. So long as he kept his head, he was safe. He mustn't let them trap him into any damaging admission. *Wary and cool*, that was his motto; *wary and cool.*

Then followed streams of questions: Why had he gone to Amchester? Did he often go? What about Miriam? What about Simon? Had he any enemies? *De mortuis* . . . and all that, but what sort of man was he? Did Adrian like him? Why not?

And then, of course, it all came out about Lucy, and how Simon had stolen her from her lawful husband Adrian. That didn't look too good, of course. But Rutherford seemed to take it all for granted, stressed nothing, and hurried over that part as if he wished to save Adrian any hurt or embarrassment. And Adrian himself was restrained and manly about the whole business. Besides, as he said, it was all such a long time ago. He admitted that he had no reason to love Simon as a man.

'And as a painter?' queried the detective.

Adrian shrugged. 'His reputation as a painter was as good as his reputation as a man was bad.'

'I didn't ask you what his reputation

was. I asked what *you* thought of his work.'

'It wasn't the style of work I admired personally, but I could appreciate its undoubted brilliance. His work was inclined to be uneven, but some of it was very fine,' he said sulkily.

From behind the desk Rutherford drew out a canvas. A magnificent, glowing painting of blossom in a Chinese vase. 'What do you think of that?' he asked.

He studied it intently for some time. At last, he spoke. 'It's beautiful,' he said, and meant it. He was thrilled to see just how good it was, and glad that Simon's 'last work' should be in his best tradition; he hadn't let him down.

'Yes,' agreed Rutherford, 'it is lovely. It reminds me of a Van Gogh. But apart from that, speaking professionally, would you have any reason to doubt that it was Mr. Short's own work?'

Blinking stupidly, Adrian shook his head speechlessly.

'Ah, you see how vast is the gulf between artist and policeman.' Rutherford was terrifyingly genial. 'From our standpoint, this isn't a work of art, but a bit of valuable evidence. This wasn't painted by Mr. Short. Though it's a wonderful imitation of his manner. I reckon it would deceive the eye of any expert — *but for one thing* ... ' He leaned back in his chair, smiling.

'What — what — ?' Adrian stammered, and the flesh seemed to melt from his huge face, leaving him shrunken and haggardly pale.

'What incalculable creatures we humans are,' mused Rutherford, lethargically philosophical. 'Wouldn't you think a man was a cold-blooded brute to paint a picture while his victim lay dead at his feet? And yet that same man was so absorbed in his creation that he gave himself away as utterly as if he had signed the picture with his own name. He did what painters have always done when they are excited; he threw away his tools and painted with his fingers. That infallible signature, the *fingerprint*, is all over this bit of canvas.'

The constable loomed enormous beside him. Dully, through the thudding darkness of the atmosphere, he heard Rutherford intone: ' ... and I must warn you that anything you say will be taken down and may be used in evidence.'

A Thing Possessed

Geologists, of course, are accustomed to measure Time in hundreds of thousands, even millions, of years. It seems quite natural to them. But geologists are also human, and a mere twenty-five years can seem a considerable span when it is the measure of nearly half one's own individual life, Katherine Pritchett thought wryly. That was how long it was since she had seen London. It struck her the more potently because she hardly recognized it, it had changed so much from the shabby old bomb-shattered city she remembered from 1947.

It was not only that the soot-blackened stone buildings now gleamed airily in the pale, pearly atmosphere; it was not only that the once scarred and dingy houses were now trim and bright with fresh paint, and there was a stream of brilliant colours ceaselessly moving through the thoroughfares; but the very shape and structure of the place seemed to have altered: roads were no longer where she remembered them, great glittering boxes stood upended to the sky where once had stood small shops or a row of terraced houses, and here and there a roundabout had swallowed up an elegant Georgian square. It gave Professor Pritchett an odd sensation. In a flash of exceptional fancy, it occurred to her that that might be how ghosts felt when they returned to earth, except that Professor Pritchett had no such irrational superstitions.

She had some difficulty locating the block of flats where the Duchemins lived, and feared she would be late. She should have taken a taxi; it had been foolish of her to walk, but the day was so fine, so spring-like . . .

Professor Duchemin had taught Political Economy at Toronto University at the same period as herself. That they were both English created a bond, and he and his wife had been very kind to her. Then the Duchemins had returned to England, and she had gone soon after to Berkeley University in California. They continued to write to one another, at least at Christmas. And when Katherine came back to London, she'd phoned them, and they had at once asked her to lunch.

Millie kissed her.

'We want to hear all about everything. Come and sit down.'

'You know what happened to Winterton at McGill, don't you?' said Harold, beginning to laugh.

'Now, don't swamp her, Harold. Let her get her breath. She's so pale. Why are you so pale, dear?'

'Am I?' said Katherine, smiling. 'I'm perfectly well.'

'You don't look it.'

'It's nothing.' She laughed. 'I had a fright just now — in Leinster Gardens.'

'Why?'

'I don't know. I've no idea.'

'But one can't be frightened without a cause, can one?' Millie observed reasonably.

'Evidently one can, Millie. It was just a wave of irrational terror, and now it's passed.'

'Well, if you say so, dear. Not a sherry,

Harold; I'm sure Katherine would rather have a brandy.'

'Sherry's fine,' Katherine protested.

'It's no good arguing with Millie, surely you remember that. If Millie says you'd rather have a brandy, that is what you must have.'

'You're very kind.'

'Men never notice anything,' said Millie, confiding a feminine glance at the other woman. She watched her swallow a little of the brandy. 'Why Leinster Gardens, I wonder? Did you live there once?'

'No, never.' She began quickly to ask Harold if the book was nearly finished, and presently Millie pottered off to the kitchen to chivvy the pans around, leaving the professors to their interminable gossip about shop.

Later, Professor Pritchett wondered why she had lied to Mrs. Duchemin. She was essentially a truthful person, not in the habit of lying to get herself out of an uncomfortable corner.

In the literal sense, it was true enough: she had never *lived* in Leinster Gardens, but —

It was so long ago, nearly half her lifetime. So deeply was the recollection buried in the lumber-room of memory that Professor Pritchett had remembered nothing about it until Millie Duchemin had started probing into the wherefore of that spasm of unreasoning fear which had shaken her as she passed through Leinster Gardens. And then it was no more than a thin edge of memory, like a light shining through a crack at the foot of a door. On leaving the Duchemins' she went back there to look for the house.

She hardly remembered what the house was like, except that it was a big Victorian terrace the yellowish-brown colour of old ivory, with steps running up to a heavy pillared porch. There had been a black-printed notice in the front window saying ROOM TO LET which had caught her eye.

It was extremely fatiguing tramping the streets to find a room that was both clean and quiet and not too depressing. This one had a broad turkey-carpeted staircase leading up to it, and the good solid furniture reminded Katherine comfortingly of her grandmother's house in

Manchester. Perhaps it was because of that, and because it was near the park, that Katherine decided it would do.

'Two pounds ten a week, payable in advance,' she remembered the landlady saying in a soft Scottish voice. 'Use of bath extra.'

Katherine must have been twenty-eight or -nine at the time: old, like a good many other people then, to start a career. But the war had caught her in the middle of her studies. There was just time to sit for her degree before she was called up. When she was demobbed, she took a six-month refresher course and then spent a year in fieldwork. After that, there seemed to be nothing for her to do, and she came to London to try and get a post as a lecturer — with any luck, somewhere abroad in a country that had not been devastated by war.

Katherine collected her cases from the station, managed to get them onto a bus, and then lugged them down the street and up the stairs to her room; where she unpacked them, shook out each garment fastidiously, and hung them in the immense satinwood wardrobe with a mirror which sent back a sallow unflattering reflection of her face. She saw in its dim recesses something dark move behind her. Or she had the impression that she saw something — but when she turned quickly, nothing was there, nothing dark like a vase or a clock on a bracket which might by an optical illusion have appeared to move. Katherine concluded that some dark bird must have flashed past the window at that moment, or perhaps the curtain had swayed in a draught.

London was a dismal city in 1947. Kathcrine found a café in the High Street that was at least warm and bright, where she ordered one of those death-defying meals to which people had become accustomed. She chose a Vienna steak, which had absolutely no connection with either Vienna or steak: it was sliced tinned meat fried in batter, but at least it was less repulsive than disguised whale meat, or that unappetising fish called snoek. If it was not actually nourishing, it filled the stomach.

A more real and satisfying nourishment was the concert Katherine went to afterwards at the Albert Hall; an extravagance she did not regret, for she returned to her lodgings feeling less despondent than she had for some time.

It was raining a fine drizzle, and her coat was quite damp when she took it off. Too damp, she thought, to put away. She hung it from the pediment of the wardrobe. But twice it fell down, slightly startling her each time as she lay reading a paperback edition of *A Passage to India*, and she was obliged to get out of bed to hook it back again. The third time, she gave in, hung it in the wardrobe, and firmly closed the door.

She read for only a little while, and then put out the light and sank into a deep and dreamless sleep. She was awakened some time later by an angry rattling noise. In that moment between waking and sleeping, it sounded to her like thunder distantly reverberating. Then she realized it was the wind shaking the window in its frame. Damn, she thought, I'll have to find something to wedge it with; I'll never be able to sleep with it like that. She uttered a petulant sigh and switched on the light. The noise ceased. All was quiet. But of course it couldn't have been the wind, for there was no wind that night.

She waited a little, and then turned off the light once more and lay down. Presently she dropped back into sleep.

The sound pierced her slumber like someone shaking her shoulder to awaken her. She started up. In the dark, to her sleep-fuddled senses, the rattling pane was like sinister laughter. She turned on the lamp again, and at once all was as quiet as before. If it was not the wind then it must be caused by the vibration of passing traffic — one of those particularly massive lorries trundling their lonely way through the night hours, perhaps.

Katherine flung back the bedclothes and went over to the window. The top of the lower frame was well above her eye-level, but she groped with her fingers for the catch. She had thought it might not be properly fastened, but it was. In fact, it was so tightly fastened that for all her efforts she could not release it. The window had evidently not been opened for years, and the catch was stiff with rust and grime. She banged the frame lightly with her fists to try and find out where the loose bit was, but it didn't budge. Oh well, she would mention it to Mrs. Macrae in the morning.

Now her hands were filthy. Katherine lifted the ewer and poured a little cold water into the basin. She was winding her hands round the soap when a flash of light from the wardrobe mirror behind her caught the corner of her eye as the door swung open. Out of the dark interior, a shapeless brown object flew towards Katherine. She eyed it, dumb-struck with terror and incomprehension. It seemed to be continuously changing its form as it advanced. It flopped to the carpet just before it reached her and lay in a crumpled heap. Almost before she had realized that it was her skirt, Katherine saw her fawn jumper whirl from the dark depths in the same way. And then another garment. And another.

Katherine stood there, her hands

slippery with soap, her head twisted over her shoulder, staring at the extraordinary phenomenon. It was exactly as if these things were being hurled at her malevolently by someone *inside* the wardrobe who was in a terrible rage. It had the effect of making Katherine feel terrified. A shoe hit her on the shoulder. She *was* being attacked.

Katherine half-turned away and shook her hands quickly in the cold water. The wardrobe was empty now. She picked up the basin and turned to empty it into the slop-pail, when she saw the turned-back sheet on the bed rise up — as though somebody was using it to masquerade as a ghost.

Katherine never could remember afterwards how she managed to get out of that room. She spent the rest of the night huddled at the top of the stairs, listening . . .

When morning came at last, she went back to pack her things. The room seemed ordinary enough by daylight. Katherine might have believed the entire episode to be the figment of a nightmare if it had not been for the disorder. Firming her will, she picked up the clothing and crushed the garments hurriedly into the cases. When she was dressed, she went downstairs and found Mrs. Macrae.

'I'm sorry, I've changed my mind. I can't stay here.'

Mrs. Macrae looked at her without speaking. Then she said slowly: 'The room wasn't comfortable?'

'It doesn't suit me.'

'Then you must have your money back,' said Mrs. Macrae, and fetched her purse. She counted out forty-three shillings and slid the money delicately towards Miss Pritchett, who met the landlady's eye with a long, considering glance, and then picked the money up.

'Thank you.'

'No. I have to thank *you*,' said Mrs. Macrae in a low voice. 'Not everyone is as nice about it.'

Katherine stared.

'You mean you *know*?' she said angrily. 'But you have no right to let the room in those circumstances.'

'It's my livelihood, miss. What would you do?'

'I wouldn't let unsuspecting people sleep there, I know that. It could kill anyone with a weak heart, or frighten a person out of their wits,' she said indignantly.

'I know. You're right, of course. I do try to exercise judgement about whom I let it to. And She doesn't always — well, She doesn't object to everyone, it seems.'

'She? You know it's a she? You have seen something, someone . . . ?'

'No. I haven't seen Her. But I know who it is,' Mrs. Macrae said, turning away. The kettle spluttered on the stove. 'Miss, you'll do me the favour of taking a cup of tea before you go; I can't let you leave like this.'

Katherine hesitated, longing only to be gone from the place, but the look of appeal in Mrs. Macrae's sad violet eyes held her back. She pulled out a chair and sat down at the kitchen table.

A grateful smile eased the landlady's strained face. She set out a place for her, whisked from beneath the grill the rasher of bacon and piece of fried bread she had been keeping warm for her own breakfast, and laid it in front of Miss Pritchett. 'It's little enough to do,' she said firmly when the young woman protested.

'But it's your ration. I can't take it.'

'I don't need it, and it would please me better to see you eat it,' she said in her precise Scottish way. She set the brown earthenware teapot on the table and seated herself behind it. Gazing down into her cup, the landlady said, on a note of quiet desperation: 'There is no one to whom I can talk about it.'

'If I were you, I think I should take some advice from those who know about such things. Why not consult the Society for Psychical Research? I'm sure they would help.'

'I don't think I could do that. I mean, once it got out that the place was haunted, no one would ever come here again. And then what would I live on?'

'Yes, I see. But you can hardly let things go on as they are either, can you?' Katherine hesitated. 'I'm not religious myself, but I rather think that if I were in your shoes, I should be tempted to try anything. Have you thought of asking some ecclesiastic to exorcise the room? That is often effective, they say.'

'I appreciate your kindly intentions, miss, and I'm afraid you will think me very difficult and stupid, but . . . ' Mrs. Macrae turned her head aside. ' . . . I couldn't bring myself to do that to her, even now. You see,' she said, drawing her finger round the contour of a dull stain on the cloth, 'who knows what *happens* to a ghost who is exorcised? We only know they are banished. But where to?' she murmured, leaving nameless questions in the air.

Katherine was chilled. Perhaps the woman was a little bit mad. Katherine really looked at her for the first time. She was quite old, fiftyish, with abundant dark hair turning grey. She must have been pretty once; she had still a certain pathetic charm. No, she was not mad: just honourable.

Katherine said: 'You speak as though you knew her.'

Mrs. Macrae nodded.

'Oh yes, I knew her, more's the pity. She was my husband's mother. She hated me from the first. She never wanted Dick to marry me. And when he died, she held me to blame. So now she revenges herself. She has tied me to the house till the day I die, because she knew there was no other way I could earn my living.'

'Could you not sell it, and perhaps buy a small business with the proceeds?'

'Under the terms of the will, I am not allowed to sell, or even let it; I am obliged to live in it, and may not even will it away. When I die, it will go to a Cats' Home.' Mrs. Macrae gave a faint laugh.

Katherine looked shocked. 'I've never heard of anything so venomous. The will ought to be contested.'

'Oh no, my dear. There's nothing to contest, even if there'd been the money to take it to court. A mother-in-law is under no obligation to provide for her son's widow. Some people might think I was lucky, and I suppose I am. Only — ' Her voice trembled. ' — I sometimes wonder how much longer I can bear it.' She smiled shakily. 'Let me give you another cup, my dear. It's done me so much good to talk to you.'

'I'm afraid I've not been of much help,' murmured Katherine, who did not believe in ghosts, though it seemed rude to say so to someone who believed herself to be haunted. Moreover, it was impossible to deny that she had been badly frightened by something. Now, in broad daylight, she began almost to doubt the validity of her own fears. 'This — this thing, that you say you've never seen — how do you know it's the ghost of your mother-in-law?'

'Why, who else would it be, dear? This is her house and that was her room. And if you had known her as I did, you would recognize her unmistakably by the way she behaves. She was always a violent and self-willed person.'

'But what would be the purpose behind this unreasoning malice?'

'Who can tell! Perhaps she doesn't even know herself. Perhaps she is no more than a blind, mindless force. Perhaps that's what being a ghost is, like a record needle stuck in a groove, playing the same notes on and on, until maybe someone releases it.'

Miss Pritchett never saw Mrs. Macrae again. But, about six months later, she was shocked to see in the paper that a Mrs. Macrae had been murdered in her home in Leinster Gardens. She went out at once and bought all the newspapers she could find.

Piecing the information together as best she could, she learned that the woman had been discovered lying in her nightclothes on a bed in an upper room, her body enveloped in a sheet with which it appeared she had been strangled. Several items of silver were missing from a cabinet. The police were anxious to contact a man believed to have stayed at the house on the night of the murder. None of the papers mentioned in which room the murder had taken place.

A week later, she read that a man was said to be helping the police with their inquiries. And forty-eight hours after that, it was reported that a thirty-two-year-old man, name of Ronald James, had been arrested for the murder of Mrs. Janet

Macrae on the night of the eighteenth of that month.

Why should the man have murdered her? Katherine thought, and tried to put the matter from her mind. But it kept creeping in and taking her unawares. If only she knew which room it had happened in . . . but she hadn't the least idea how she could go about finding out, for she was in Nottingham at the time. And anyway, there was nothing she could do, was there? If the man was innocent, he would be released. If he was guilty, then it was better she should not interfere. It really was none of her business.

Ronald James was committed for trial at the Old Bailey. A force stronger than her own judgement took Katherine to London, the college having broken up for the long vacation.

The house in Leinster Gardens was closed up, and something about its desolate appearance brought the reality of the situation home to her as nothing else had. It was no longer just a newspaper story: it was true. Seeing her staring up at it from the other side of the road, a woman paused beside her, and, with a residue of communicativeness left over from the war, announced: 'You can't see the room from this side; it was at the back. I mean, if that's your interest in the house.'

'I knew Mrs. Macrae.'

'Oh? Poor soul! A terrible thing to happen to anyone, whatever they may have done. But I always say it's asking for trouble for a woman alone to let rooms to single men. Still, being a widow, she would have been lonely. I'm not blaming her,' said the woman quickly, 'it's not for us to judge one another, is it? I know what it's like, having lost mine.'

Katherine said stiffly:

'I don't know what you're talking about.'

'Don't mind me. It's none of my business, after all. But you can't get away from the fact that she was in her nightie when they found her, dead, in the man's bed on the second floor back. It speaks for itself, doesn't it?'

There was no need for Katherine to

listen to any more, once she had learned that the murder had taken place in the 'second floor back'. It meant she *had* to do something. She went to the police and said she had some information for the defence in the case of Rex *v* James, and could they put her in touch with the accused's solicitor?

'Miss Pritchett?' said Mr. Ableman, the solicitor, a smooth, middle-aged, balding gentleman, rising from behind his desk to greet her. 'Do sit down. I understand you have some information for us concerning our client, Ronald James.'

'I believe he is innocent.'

'So do we,' said Mr. Ableman suavely.

But she knew that he didn't mean it. This smooth gentleman would never believe anyone to be innocent. And suddenly Katherine felt herself to be old-maidish, ridiculous, provincial — seeing herself through his sophisticated, superior eyes. She pulled off her gloves and loosened her coat.

'It is a difficult story to tell,' she began. 'But I want you to listen to what happened to me in that room on the second floor back a few months ago.'

Mr. Ableman put his fingertips together and listened quite patiently. She had feared he would laugh. But he didn't. When she had finished, he was silent for a moment or two, and then he said:

'It was good of you to come, Miss Pritchett. It can't have been easy. And you mustn't think I doubt the veracity of your story. I am sure it happened exactly as you say. But you are an intelligent woman, and you must see that one could not put it forward as a feasible defence. It would simply be laughed out of court. It assumes too much. It is asking rather a lot of anyone to believe that an intangible ghost — always supposing there really are such things — could have the physical strength to strangle anyone.'

'It requires power, not physique. It was the *sheet* that strangled her, don't you see?'

'I'm sorry,' said Mr. Ableman, shaking his head.

'You're not going to do anything about it then? Even though it may mean an innocent man will be hanged.'

'I have great faith in British Justice,' said Mr. Ableman, bowing.

Katherine was in court on the first day of Ronald James's trial. She listened to the prosecution's counsel outlining the case against the prisoner to the ladies and gentlemen of the jury. It was through the pieces of silver he alleged he had bought from the murdered woman that he had been traced. He alleged that he had paid Mrs. Macrae twenty-five pounds for the teapot, milk jug, and silver salver, but the money was never found. (And so on and so forth.)

Ronald James sat in the dock, looking as unperturbed as though all this had nothing to do with him. He was a handsome little man, with a jaunty, sensual, conceited expression. If looks were anything to go by, he might well be guilty.

At any rate, they hanged him.

Professor Pritchett stared up at the vast office building standing where once the Victorian houses had been. She was glad the house was no longer there. The ghost must have departed with it: ghosts can hardly haunt modern offices, there could be nothing for them to do in those bleak functional edifices. The sheer unreasoning terror which had struck her earlier as she passed through must have only been the long-forgotten memory rising unbidden from some deep recess in her mind. Mustn't it?

Captain Jenkins and
Amadeo Smith

The following MS was found folded in a cheap edition of Sterne's 'Sentimental Journey', on a Nothing-Over-Sixpence tray in Charing Cross Road. I thought it had the ring of truth about it. I was most struck by the agitation of the handwriting: it had plainly been written under great emotional stress.

* * *

Why am I writing this? Because I cannot tell what the next few hours may bring? I cannot foresee what will take place? It must be some such reason, for I am not given to talking about myself; but now, under the impetus of pending doom, I want you to understand everything.

If I can only make you understand the trouble I have been through, the immense burdens that have been placed on my shoulders. Not that that in itself . . . Ah, how to begin my story! It all seems so far away now — it recedes as I approach, slips from my grasp like a thin, emerald eel. I *must* . . . If only I could hold my thought. Everything is roaring down a black abyss and I am left, clutching the wind.

You think I am mad? Ah, if you knew how wrong you are, how far from the truth. Yes, I am a little incoherent, but that is because of the wind tonight. The rain is moaning and beating against the windows; the wind keeps shrieking in agony: 'Let me in. For pity's sake let me in. Oh, oh, oh!'

I hate to hear the wind so alive; the whole house is alive tonight, everything creaking and moving — and I am alone. I admit I am frightened — who could be otherwise in the circumstances? My heart is beating so loudly that the air seems full of the sound of wings. Look how violently my hand trembles. I can hardly guide the pen.

The *things* are trying to daunt me, but I shall not turn my hand from the task I have set before it.

I am in my forty-third year . . . is that to the point? I must not squander these precious flying minutes by writing irrelevancies. No, what manner of man I am is unimportant, nor could I describe myself truthfully now, since I fear . . . I dare not write, nor mouth, nor even *think* of what I fear. I am *not* mad, I beg you not to think me mad. Believe me, it would be much better if I were.

Perhaps the whole thing is my fault; had I been less shy and timid as a child, more responsive to overtures of friendship, more open-hearted and generous of character, then my story might have been different. No matter, though. I *was* a silent, reserved child, mainly because my parents enjoined such caution in me. Although I had an instinctively affectionate and confiding nature, one or two early experiences soon taught me a Spartan, disciplined self-control which served me faithfully, never forsaking me until the forty-first year of my life. Ah, that cursed, cursed day!

What was that noise? Nothing, nothing; a branch tapping its dirt-soiled, skeleton fingers against the glass pane. You must not mind me being so nervous — it is the shrill dark of the night, and I feel so helpless . . .

I was saying that I was reserved. Yes, in spite of the troubles and anxieties I have been through, or perhaps I should say *because* of these anxieties, I became more taciturn with the passing years.

Although outwardly I appeared confident and self-reliant, inwardly I was tortured with doubts, and my heart was heavy with loneliness, remorse and dread. Sometimes in the monotonous white dawns I have thought my heart would burst with the longing for a friend to share my pain. There was no-one.

With the years my burdens increased, and as they did so, it became more impossible to find a confidant. It would have been too dangerous. I dared not speak, there was none I could trust. No, not even to my wives dared I speak in the warm silences of the night, dearly though I loved them. It was at those times, when my silent endurance was failing, that, full of unshed tears and bitter passion, I tore myself from their tender embraces for ever, adding yet another load of remorse to my weary shoulders.

I will not weary you with the listed details of my woes. My crimes are too numerous and too varied in value to be presented here. So much I have done, and so much I have left undone; yet nothing of that time has any significance now. None of that weighs on my conscience now, because . . .

(Stop! Oh, this unceasing vigilance — only just in time. I thought — I thought the room was shrinking before my eyes, closing darkly about me, the furniture bending over in a swart embrace . . . I just raised my eyes in time. You understand why I am nervous now; I have little enough power left to stay the forces of the inanimate — even less those of the elements. If I am not constantly on guard they will surround and overpower me. I find it very exhausting to be so watchful . . .)

I must hurry. In my forty-first year I met this man. Should I tell his name? Yes, yes, yes. His name is Amadeo Smith.

Amadeo Smith! (No, he won't come to my call, *I* must go to *him*.) Listen to the villainous sound of the ebbing syllables. I should not have been deceived by their softness, but I was. Besides, he seemed such a gentle, unharmful creature, with his silky, mouse-coloured hair falling over his smooth, white brow; his mournful gazelle-like eyes and the outward thrust of his delicate jaw; he was as touchingly hopeful as a child. He seemed, from the moment we met, to cling to me, to shelter appealingly against my bluff exterior. He invited me — nay, begged me — to visit him at once and for as long a period as I could bear. I — I accepted his generous offer. I liked him, so why not?

The life was comfortable enough in all conscience, and he proved a thoughtful, considerate host. He was, he told me, a writer. The subject of his work? Why, just tales; tales of real life, tales made on the stuff which lies beneath men's flesh and bones.

Nothing more than that? What could so pale and youthful a man know of what lay beneath the flesh of another? I sighed.

It was, he said, part instinct and part an acquired art to feel at the mind of another. He said he had recognised immediately that mine was a strange, tormented character full of unresolved problems — that was why he had been impelled to offer friendship to a stranger. 'I believe,' he said, 'that I can help you . . . ' and much more to that effect, all in the gentlest, most tactful manner.

I believed him, against my better judgement. I believed him. At last I agreed to try and tell him my story.

At first it was hard, it was agonising. The words lay like a mighty seal on my tongue. He sat opposite me, silent as a mummy, his great melancholy eyes wide and blank, staring dumbly into mine . . . Thus we passed many still hours, in violent, wordless battle. Then one day I spoke freely, as simply as a child. Ah, the joy, the first exquisite sense of relief! At last the sharing of my burden; I could feel my soul lightening . . .

(The wind has dropped. Do you hear how still the world is now? So still that I can hear the stars swinging through space. The noise of my pen is unendurable, like the scratching of ancient Chinese nails on a coffin lid . . .)

At the beginning, I was happy and at peace. I felt I was merely talking aloud to myself, so still and silent was my companion. Never by word or sign did he betray emotion at my tale — sometimes I wondered if he heard, if he was not in some far dream country of his invention. He *was* listening; for as my tale proceeded, he would sometimes scratch a brief note on the pad that lay before him. No other sign than that; no comment of pity, approbation or disapproval ever marred his countenance.

Gradually, the lightening of my soul turned to a sullen emptiness. Why was I trusting this stranger with my secret heart? Had he an Olympian right to his calm pose? What did I gain from this *triste* venture? I missed my privacy of thought, I grew to hate him; but now there was no escape; he knew me better than I knew myself, I could not hide from him.

One day he came to me and said I was

free to go if I liked. He thanked me for taking pity on his solitude for so long, but now he had no further need of me. *He* gave me leave to go! . . . I left as swiftly as I could.

(Why is the night suddenly so quiet? I cannot bear it! It is as if the room, the bare trees, the torn clouds, the very air were tense, taut, breathless . . . waiting for something. Oh, *what* are they waiting for? This static is too much . . .)

When I had said goodbye to Amadeo Smith I felt a queer, blank emptiness drop over me. It was as if nothing was left — no, more than that — as if something was missing. I felt as a man must feel when he has lost his memory . . . void and fearful. This horrid sensation of vacancy increased from day to day. I wondered if people noticed it; I believed they did. People seemed not to see me, or rather to see right through me as they would a vacuous glass. Walking in the street I was wary to keep away from crowds, fearing they would unseeingly walk through me, breaking the brittle shell of transparency that was my body.

Day by day my hold on reality became more tenuous. Yesterday I saw my face reflected in a piece of mirror-glass. Oh, horror, horror! There were no pupils to my eyes — *there were no eyes!* From the empty sockets shone a piercing white light . . . whiter than the blind eyes of a statue. I felt as cold as a ghost at this awful vision of my poor uninhabited body. Horrid, horrid sight! You understand that there is not a moment to lose if I am to be saved. There is a rushing in my ears. The blood roars round and round my empty skull. I must go at once to Amadeo Smith and *force* him to give me back my mind, my mind, my soul, that he has stolen. He will give it back to me, won't he?

Capt. Chas. Jenkins.

★ ★ ★

The MS ended there. What had happened? Who was Captain Jenkins? I decided to find out if I could. Unfortunately, the MS was undated, and I could only make the vaguest guess as to the period. The bookseller proved useless, which didn't surprise me — it was only a cheap edition and must have passed through many hands. My next job was to trace a Capt. Chas. Jenkins of (probably) the nineteenth century. I had not expected this to be so fruitless: both the Naval Records and the Merchant Service seem to have been entirely captained by Jenkinses at that time. Eventually I turned to Amadeo Smith, unhopefully. After much tiresome investigation and endless queries I found him. At least, I found a cutting of the *Colchester Courier* dated 3rd Feb., 1854. It read:

A man, later identified as Amadeo Smith, was found last night in Honeypool Lane. He had been notified as missing for some days, and when found appeared to be exhausted from exposure. At the station he stubbornly refused to remove the steel helmet he wore, iterating that some person or persons wished to pluck out his mind. He was certified and removed to Colchester Asylum.

The Follower

(The following notes are taken from the doctor's case book, in which she is called simply Mrs. S.)

Every day at 6.35 p.m. Mrs. S., twenty-nine years of age and happily married, breaks into a flood of weeping. This quotidian event has been taking place regularly for more than two months. That is, almost five weeks before her case came up and she was sent here for treatment.

Prior to this, for the past year, Mrs. S. has been subject to deep psychological disturbances, though showing no neurotic symptoms previously. Her earlier history indicates a well-balanced normal personality.

The crying attacks are of course merely a symptom of her inner distress. Whether she is alone or among people seems to make no difference to the spasm of weeping; it appears to be involuntary.

Before she came here, Mrs. S. once or twice went to a cinema in the hope that the story unfolding before her eyes would so absorb her attention that the moment would pass unremarked and the spell be broken. It did not work. In the middle of some hilarious comedy, in the middle of her own laughter even, she told me, sobs would rise in her throat, tears burst from her eyes, and she would struggle past the serried knees in the darkness to the seclusion of the lavatory.

Of course, Mrs. S. does not trust me. Which is only to be expected in the circumstances. She has lost faith in doctors, naturally. She no longer looks to them for help in her predicament. It is safe to say that she would not be here if she were not obliged to. Being a sensible woman, she does try to cooperate as far as she can. But it is difficult to help a patient on such terms. Doubly difficult when one does not oneself know how to interpret what happened. To interpret the *meaning* of what she experienced, that is.

I do not suppose there is a rational explanation. The best I can do is to assure her that she was not mad, is not mad now, and is not going mad. I suggest that what happened perhaps occurred in another dimension of Time. She is really still too young to have become aware of the complex mystery of Time. She takes it for granted like the air she breathes. In simple terminology, I described to her how man's idea of the universe in which he lives is wholly subject to the limitations of his senses and perceptions. Which is why we think of Time as one-dimensional, flowing always in one direction, from the past to the future, like a river. But suppose, I put it to her, there should be other dimensions to Time? Suppose Time ran in even two directions at once, like a moving staircase? Only, instead of gliding up and down like that mechanism, the movement of Time runs from the future to the past as well as from the past to the future.

She does not seem to make much of the notion at present. But the seed has been sown and one day perhaps will germinate.

(A page from Mrs. S.'s diary, dated February 18th.)

I have been here ten weeks. Only ten weeks! Another nine months and two weeks still to go. *Do I get time off for good behaviour?* I asked Dr Braceridge. And he said — as I knew he would — 'This isn't a prison, you know.'

He wants me to write down an account of the affair from the beginning. The very thought of it makes me feel sick. But now every time I see him he asks me what progress I'm making with it. I tell him, none.

He gazes at me sorrowfully.

'I've tried,' I tell him. Which is the truth. 'But I can't do it. I can't get it down.'

'Try again, there's a good girl.'

I can't see the point. I've told it to him so often that he must know it as well as I do.

'I don't want you to write it for *me*,' he adds.

216

'Then for who? You can't want it for the magistrate, surely. And the police have had a statement. Who else is concerned?'

'Forget about the magistrate. Forget about the police. Forget about me. Just put down on paper, quite simply and without exaggeration, everything you remember as it occurred. I want you to try to recollect it as it seemed to you while it was happening — which will not be at all the way you think and feel about it now.'

'What good will that do? What is past is past. We can't alter it.'

'Funnily enough, that is just what we can do. We look back, and it seems to us that a particular period of our lives was very happy or a certain experience very miserable; but ten years later we may see it quite differently. The past alters according to how we see it in the present.'

'But the facts will not be changed.'

'No, the facts will not be changed. But what may be changed is your interpretation of them.'

'I doubt it,' I say bitterly. 'And how could that help?'

'If we can understand what really happened, we may learn how to come to terms with it.'

To come to terms with it. That is what I have to do. I know it. I stare down at my nails, well-kept and palely gleaming, and for some reason I suddenly recall the feel of his little hand in mine.

'I'll have another shot.' My voice comes out small and husky.

'Good.' He stands up, to show me the session is over. But as I pass through the door, he adds: 'You might find it easier to write in the third person, as though you were writing about someone else or even telling a story that had never happened at all.'

In the end, that was how I did it.

* * *

The first time Mrs. Sale saw him was in the supermarket. It is significant that her attention was drawn to him by another person. The woman laid a gloved finger lightly on Mrs. Sale's wrist and said with a smile:

'I think your little boy is looking for you.'

Mrs. Sale, naturally, turned her head in the direction of the woman's glance, and perceived at the far end of the long brightly-lit aisle a solid little red-haired boy gazing straight at her. When her eye caught his, she had the extraordinary impression that he recognised her, that he was about to come pounding up to her. Which was absurd, of course, because she had never seen him before in her life. Of that, she was quite certain. Mrs. Sale gave him a surprised look and turned away with a smile.

'He doesn't belong to me, I'm afraid.'

'I'm sorry,' said the woman, embarrassed, feeling a fool. 'I do beg your pardon. It was the way he was looking at you. I felt sure . . . '

'Yes, he was, wasn't he? Probably only thinking what a funny hat I'm wearing.' She laughed. 'You know what kids are.' Mrs. Sale glanced over her shoulder to verify his expression, but the child was no longer there. She shrugged. The women smiled at one another with a mixture of amusement and awkwardness, and separated.

That concluded the incident. It disappeared at once from Mrs. Sale's mind into the limbo of memory where the past lies higgledy-piggledy, like junk in an attic, waiting to be discovered again. Treasures and trivia may lie there for years, may lie there unwanted for ever; may be searched for and not found, or may be wanted again almost at once. It turned up very quickly for Mrs. Sale. Though it was not until much later — months later, in fact — that she remembered the child had first been seen by this other woman. By that time Mrs. Sale would have given a great deal to know who she was; but, as might be expected, she never saw her again.

★   ★   ★

A couple of days later, on her way to take her dog for a run on the common, Mrs. Sale noticed a child playing in the road outside her house. She did not actually recognize him as the boy in the supermarket, but something about his concentrated gaze as he eyed her stirred some vague recollection in her mind.

'Hullo,' she said. 'I've seen you before, haven't I?'

He did not return her smile, just gazed at her over the rim of the ball he was pressing against his mouth as though it was an orange. Mrs. Sale guessed him to be about seven years of age. And evidently shy. She had the curious impression that his deep-fringed stare was accusatory, but that was nonsense.

Trotter, the dog, was behaving very oddly, straining at the end of his lead and uttering shrill, nervous barks. The little boy tried to preserve his imperturbable air, but she observed that he flinched minutely and took a small step backwards.

'Be quiet, Trot!' Mrs. Sale said sternly. 'Behave yourself! What's the *matter* with you?' And she added reassuringly above the dog's frantic yelps: 'He won't hurt you, dear. Don't be afraid ... Stop it, Trot, stop it! Isn't he a bad dog?' she cried, winding the lead tightly round her hand as the dog began to growl deep in his chest and his hackles rose. She dragged the hysterical Trotter quickly away.

Before the week was out, she saw the boy again.

'We do keep meeting, don't we!' Mrs. Sale exclaimed. 'Do you live round here?'

The boy shook his head slowly from side to side; or perhaps he was merely brushing his lips sensuously against the rubber ball (which he held pressed to his nose as before): it was impossible to tell.

'What's your name?' Mrs. Sale asked in her friendly way.

Answer came there none.

'Cat got your tongue?' inquired Mrs. Sale perkily.

No smile was mirrored back at her from his grave little face.

'Oh, come on! You must have a name, otherwise how do they call you in when it's time for tea?' Still the dark unblinking gaze held hers. 'Bet I can guess it. It's — it's Tommy Jehoshaphat!'

His eyes slid to one side. He rubbed his right ear with his shoulder.

'Well, Tommy, I mustn't stand here all day listening to your chatter,' Mrs. Sale said in her jokey manner; 'you must forgive me if I tear myself away.'

She walked off briskly, and was surprised to hear light steps running after her. Funny little boy, she thought, and decided to take no notice. Mrs. Sale walked on without looking round, and was not aware of the moment when the footsteps ceased.

* * *

Another time, she saw him with his arm around a lamp-post, wistfully watching some neighbourhood children at play. There was something pathetic about the small lonely figure. It struck her for the first time what a solitary child he was. Poor little boy, she thought. But she did not think, as many other childless women would, 'Just the sort of little boy I'd like to have!' Mrs. Sale was not a sentimentalist.

'Hey!' she called to the children, interrupting their raucous screams of excitement. 'Why don't you ask that other little boy to play? He'd like to. I think he's new here and he's feeling lonely.'

They stared at her blankly. One of them said: 'Who is?'

'That little boy over there. By the lamp-post.'

They stared, then looked at one another uncertainly. Someone broke into a smothered giggle. As if it was a signal, they suddenly made off, like a herd of small animals startled at their grazing, and as they disappeared round the corner there came the sound of a great bellow of laughter. Mrs. Sale was mystified. Tommy Jehoshaphat had vanished too, she observed.

For the first time, she mentioned the child to her husband over dinner that evening.

'I don't know who he belongs to. There must be some new people round here who I've not heard about yet. But — it's rather sweet, Neil — he seems to have taken a fancy to me; he follows me about.'

'What's his name?'

'I don't know. I call him Tommy Jehoshaphat.'

'Poor child!'

'It's only a joke.'

'So I should hope.'

'He's always by himself. A very solitary child — like Lucy Gray. I suppose that's why he follows me about, because I talk to him.'

Her husband looked up at her suddenly.

'Why isn't he at school?'

It was like her husband to put his finger instantly on the one odd factor in a given situation. She was amazed that she had not thought of it herself.

'It never occurred to me. No wonder he's lonely. Why *isn't* he at school? He doesn't look as if he's been ill; he's a sturdy little fellow.' A dreadful thought flashed across her mind. 'I do hope . . . '

'What?' said her husband, after a moment's silence showed him that she did not mean to finish the sentence.

Mrs. Sale said reluctantly:

'He never speaks, Neil. Do you think he could be . . . ? It would be too awful

225

'. . . if he were dumb or deaf.'

'Not very likely that he'd be allowed to run around the streets by himself, if he were,' Mr. Sale said sensibly,

So it could not be that. There must be some other explanation.

Sunday morning, Neil always cleaned the car. Mrs. Sale understood that for him it was an essential rite, the way other people go to church. It was his act of devotion, of worship, of praise. To see him so serious and absorbed gave her always a warm little rush of tenderness. It was charming, like watching a child imitating some grave, grown-up ploy.

She padded softly out to him and lightly kissed the back of his neck.

'That's nice,' he said. 'Two pints, please.'

'Does the milkman kiss you too?'

'Only on Saturdays.'

'Today happens to be Sunday.'

'So it is. I thought there was something different about his kiss — no moustache, of course.' His polish in one hand and a dirty rag in the other, he took her neck gently between his forearms and drew her to him. She put her arms round him and held him close.

It was a lovely May morning, sparkling and fresh as though the world had just been created, every tree dressed to kill in a diaphanous garb sprinkled with flecks of bright green. It was a day to be happy.

'Would you like to do something for me?' Neil murmured in her ear.

'If it's to help you polish the car, no,' she said quickly, slipping out of his embrace.

A rook cawed its way back to its nest on the other side of the road, and she followed it with her eyes: it would be a good summer, they were nesting high this year. She nudged her husband. 'There he is.'

'Who?'

'My follower. Look.'

'Where?'

'There, by the oak.'

'I don't see him.'

'You're looking right at him.'

'There's no one there.'

'Neil, don't be idiotic. He's looking straight at us. A little boy with red hair, wearing blue jeans.' She waved to him. 'See?' she said to her husband.

He eyed her strangely.

'There's no one there,' he repeated.

'What's the matter with you?' she cried. 'You've got eyes in your head, haven't you?'

'I've got eyes.'

'Then why can't you see him?'

'I suppose because he isn't there.'

'Damn you, you obstinate pig! How is it that *I* can see him?'

'I don't know.'

'I'll fetch him, then.'

She ran down to the gate and across the road to the line of trees cresting the bank. But he was no longer there. He had gone. She called, 'Tommy!' — just once. Then turned and walked back to the garden. She did not look at her husband; she went into the house without a word.

Mrs. Sale didn't speak to her husband for the rest of the day. He didn't understand. He thought she was sulking childishly, but she was feeling deeply shocked and bewildered. How could the little boy not have been there? And, if he was there, why couldn't Neil see him? If he *wasn't* there, how could she have seen him — not once, but half a dozen times?

'Dearest girl,' her husband said softly in bed that night, 'why are you punishing me? It's not my fault that I can't see your fantasies.' She turned towards him silently and laid her head on his shoulder.

* * *

Coming home from the library a few days later, Mrs. Sale suddenly became aware of light steps pattering behind her, and somehow intuitively she knew whose they were. She walked on, not daring to turn her head. For if he were truly a figment of her imagination, she must be ill in her mind, crazy . . . She heard a 'plop', and from the corner of her eye she saw the old red-and-blue ball teeter to the kerb edge and roll into the gutter. She stooped and picked it up — still warm and grubby from his hands. It was firm, real, three-dimensional. A queer wave of relief swept over her. She turned. 'Here!' she said, and lobbed it gently into Tommy

Jehoshaphat's grimy outstretched paws.

When she collected her husband from the station that evening, she put it to him: 'Could one touch a fantasy?'

'What?' he said.

'Would a fantasy be solid to the touch, Neil? I imagined it would be insubstantial, like a ghost.'

'I'm not with you.'

'I saw him again today.'

'Who?'

'The boy . . . the boy you couldn't see,' she added impatiently.

'Oh . . . And you touched him.'

'I picked up his ball. It was still warm from his hands. I couldn't have imagined that, could I?'

'Then I must have been wrong. Don't become neurotic about it, darling.'

'I'm just glad to know I didn't invent him out of a disordered subconscious, or something.'

*   *   *

But something highly disagreeable — quite uncanny, in fact — occurred soon

230

afterwards. Once again on an empty stretch of road she became aware of small feet scurrying after her. 'Hullo, Tommy,' she began to say as she swung round ... She felt the blood drain from her cheeks: *no one was there.*

'Don't be silly,' Mrs. Sale said to herself in sharp reproof, 'you just imagined you heard him.' And she walked on with a firm tread, listening to the steady beat of her steps on the pavement ...

Between each of her steps there was the sound of two or three small skipping steps, as if someone were dancing along beside her ...

Mrs. Sale began to run ...

★   ★   ★

The climax came one morning as she returned from the shops. It was a day of high summer. Mrs. Sale was wearing a sleeveless blue dress with short white gloves. Even they were too hot, and she took them off and dropped them into her basket. As she crossed the road, a child's hand slid into hers — deliciously soft, warm and alive. A curiously tender sensation. She glanced quickly down at her side, and her heart gave a great lurch, as though she had fallen over a step that wasn't there. *The space beside her was empty.* She was alone. But the child's hand was still in hers. She could feel the little bones crunching in her tightening grasp.

★　★　★

When Neil arrived home, he saw at once that she was ill and he sent for their doctor. To him she poured it all out in an hysterical flood, knowing he would not laugh or disbelieve her. 'What is the matter with me?' she cried. 'Is he real or is he not real? Is he a ghost or am I having hallucinations?'

The doctor spoke of 'nerves' and advised a change of scene. Mrs. Sale went to stay with her sister for a fortnight in the Channel Islands. She did not mention her mysterious trouble. She tried to put it out of her mind. But it did no good. As soon as she was back, it all started up again, just as she had expected it would.

'What have I done to this child that he should haunt me like this? Why *me*?' she cried in despair to her husband, her face haggard.

Her husband objected to the word *haunted*. He was a materialist and did not believe in ghosts.

But she *was* haunted, Mrs. Sale insisted. 'It makes me feel like an empty room in which something dreadful happened a long time ago.'

Her husband found the idea extremely distasteful; he did not like his sensible girl becoming neurotic and fanciful. He urged his wife to see a psychiatrist (psychiatrists don't believe in ghosts either). A good psychiatrist would soon get to the root of the trouble, and cure her of this tiresome obsession that was taking all the fun out of their life.

Dr Williams, the psychiatrist, was in accord with her husband that the hallucinations were an obsession. They were a projection from a split in her own personality — caused, no doubt, by guilt or fear. Their task, he explained to her, would be to find out what the reason was for her hidden guilt and fear — a guilt so intense, he assured her, that she had (quite unconsciously, of course) separated herself from it at the expense of the integration of her personality. In order to be able to live with herself, she had externalized it as a thing outside herself: thus disintegrating her personality. It made Mrs. Sale quake with dread to think what had to be discovered.

It came out, during their long backward groping into the past, that some seven or eight years previously Mrs. Sale had had an abortion.

'Now we have it,' said Dr Williams with quiet satisfaction. 'You are being haunted by your hidden sense of guilt at having killed your unborn child.'

His complete assurance that he had solved the problem disconcerted Mrs. Sale, who had not known she had felt any guilt at all: at the time, it had simply seemed to her the only thing possible. She felt coarse and insensitive and ashamed of herself for *not* having suffered guilt. Dr Williams explained to her that her guilt had been so deeply repressed that she had been unaware of it.

Little by little, he convinced her of the truth of what he said. He made her understand that the child did not exist; never had existed. She realized now that not only had the child not been apparent to Neil, but the neighbourhood children had not seen him either. Yet he had been perfectly real, unquestionably *there*, to the woman in the supermarket who had drawn her attention to him at the beginning.

The child in the supermarket may have been there, the doctor conceded, which was why he had served as the starting-point for her obsession. Seeing the child there, at that particular moment, gave an identity, a physical presence, to the ghost of an unborn child which was haunting her subconscious. Thereafter, the ghost in her mind became externalized into a boy child of just the age her own child would have been had it been allowed to live.

That was why, said the doctor, he always seemed to be following *her*, always seemed to be looking at *her*, as though he was trying to convey something to her; because he was the projection of her own subconscious.

'I didn't notice it at the time,' said Mrs. Sale. 'Only afterwards I had the impression he had been trying to tell me something important, something urgent . . . Poor little ghost!'

'What you have to understand, Mrs. Sale, is that the urgent, unhappy message you felt was coming from the child — or ghost, or hallucination, or however you like to think of him — was issuing from your own mind, your own subconscious anxiety . . . '

At the end of three months, Mrs. Sale returned home, cured. Mr. and Mrs. Sale began to be happy again, as they had been before her curious obsession began.

Autumn was late that year. It was the end of October before the leaves began to fall, drifting slowly through the sunlit air in gleams of orange and scarlet and blood-red . . .

Mrs. Sale was driving to the station to collect her husband. They were having some friends in to dinner, and her mind was occupied with charming domestic details for a successful evening, while her eyes kept watch on the familiar route. An old woman crossed the road slowly with a fat white dog. A Spider Fiat cut in dangerously between herself and a ten-ton lorry. Twenty yards ahead, a child in blue jeans with red hair was bouncing a red-and-blue ball on the pavement. She recognized him instantly. It was Tommy Jehoshaphat, the ghost-child, the figment of her mind that she had thought never to see again. She had been told she was cured, that the poison of her suppressed guilt had been drawn out of her like a decayed tooth. She frantically assured herself that there was nothing to fear; but she was trembling.

The ball bounced into the road, and the little boy rushed after it as though at all costs he must save the ball from harm.

There might have been time to brake. But that would have meant that she thought the child was real. And she knew he was not. She knew he simply was not there, and she refused to believe in him. Mrs. Sale clenched her teeth and pressed her foot hard down on the accelerator.

She felt the bump as she hit him. She heard a woman scream. She braked. People began to run towards her. With shaking legs, Mrs. Sale somehow walked round to the front of the car. She knelt down. She touched him. There was blood on the edge of her skirt. She could not understand how a hallucination could be so real. A policeman lifted her to her feet. She heard someone say, 'He's dead.' So *they* could see him too.

* * *

In court, witnesses stated that the driver had appeared to accelerate and drive deliberately straight at the child.

Mrs. Sale was heard to say in a faint voice that she had believed the child was not really there.

'They told me he wasn't real,' she kept saying. 'They said I had imagined him.'

Dr Williams testified that he had been treating Mrs. Sale for a psychological disorder. It was, he thought, an unfortunate coincidence that the child who had been killed had resembled the child in Mrs. Sale's obsession. He could offer no other explanation of what had occurred.

No one could explain it to Mrs. Sale. Rational persons who do not believe in ghosts are hardly likely to accept that one could be haunted by the ghost of someone one had not yet killed.

But Mrs. Sale believed that that was what he had been trying to tell her. And she had not understood. Poor little boy. There was nothing she could do now but weep for him every evening at the hour he died.

Crooked Harvest

Nigel Armstrong wondered disconsolately why he had ever imagined that a quiet holiday in the country would be fun. It was dull, unbearably dull. No one to talk to, nothing to do but walk. He kicked an inoffensive stone along the lane. It wasn't true that country folk were friendly, they were hatefully reserved and stuck up. That adorably pretty Miss Brown, for instance. Her house was a stone's throw from his, they saw each other daily, and yet he could not get into conversation with her.

He leant against a convenient stile and lit his pipe, his strong brown hands cupping the little flame protectively. Why wouldn't the girl speak to him? Was he a leper or something? They could have had such fun together, there were so many things *two* people could do — why, even walking was enjoyable if you had a companion. And she looked such a darling. He mused idiotically about her cute trick of blushing when he said good morning to her; and then passed easily into a daydream wherein he rescued her from a burning house, or a bull, or — oh, there were hundreds of variations — and thereby earned her undying gratitude.

He walked on, immersed in his dream. The faint humming in the distance became a sudden roar in his ears. Instinctively, he flung himself into the hedge. The huge, cream-coloured car flashed past him and disappeared round the bend.

'Brute!' muttered Nigel, and wiped his forehead. 'Coming at that speed down a country lane.'

When Nigel arrived back at his little cottage, he saw the cream-coloured roadster standing outside Miss Brown's gate. There was something vaguely familiar about it. Could it be — ? No, it was ridiculous to think of it. There must be hundreds of cream Sandham Super Twelves on the road. His eyes puckered at the corners as they strained to read the number-plate.

He exhaled in a long-drawn whistle. So it *was* Oscar Thark's car! He bit savagely on his pipe-stem as he recalled how Thark had swindled him a few short weeks ago. Thark had walked into Nigel's little antique shop as cool as an iceberg — and just about as dangerous — chosen something, paid for it on the spot, and walked away. It was only later, when the shop was shut and Nigel was making up his books, that he discovered the notes he had been paid with were counterfeit. He had wasted much time and money in trying to trace Oscar Thark — and now to run into him in this absurdly unpopulated spot! The gods were indeed sportive! Were they playing into his hands at last? he wondered.

But what was his car doing outside Judy Brown's cottage? Was he a friend of hers? Did she know he was a crook? Obviously she didn't, or he wouldn't be there. Well, why *was* he there? Supposing he was up to his tricks again? Something, Nigel decided, must be done about this. He must let the girl know what she was up against. But how? You couldn't just walk into a girl's house and say, 'Hullo! I just dropped in to tell you that your friend is a crook.' No, it wasn't done.

Funny to think that barely an hour ago he was inventing dozens of ways of rescuing her from peril, and now that a most unpleasant peril was sitting in her best armchair he couldn't think of a thing to do about it. Life was like that, he decided bitterly.

Hastily, he bolted some lunch, his mind still groping for a solution. No good! He straightened his tie, smoothed back his rumpled hair, and rose to his feet. He would have to trust to the inspiration of the moment, that was all.

His long legs covered the short distance between the two houses in a few minutes. The gate squealed hideously as he pushed it open and strode up the little path.

She must have heard the gate, for the door opened before he had time to knock. She gazed at him, her brown eyes wide with surprise, one small hand clenched at her side.

Gosh! She looked sweet in that little

flowered dress. He swallowed convulsively. 'Miss Brown, I hardly — well, I don't — but we are neighbours, aren't we? You see — er — oh, Lord, you must believe me — ' It was harder than he had imagined. He hadn't felt such a fool since he'd gone up to collect the Scripture Prize on Speech Day; then, too, his hands had swollen up like balloons and his tongue had felt like a lump of boiled flannel.

The girl smiled. 'What is it, Mr. — ?'

'Armstrong, Nigel Armstrong,' he supplied hastily. 'Look here, you're going to think this the most awful bit of cheek, I know. But — ' He was stuck again. He ran a finger desperately round the inside of his collar.

'Do you think you could be a little more explicit, Mr. Armstrong? You see, I have somebody waiting inside . . . ' She blushed delightfully, as if she had been over-bold in speaking to this strange male creature.

'But it's just about that that I'm here,' he said eagerly. 'Do you know who that man is? Miss Brown, I don't know if he's a friend of yours or a complete stranger, but I do beg you to be careful, very careful.'

'Careful!' she echoed. 'Careful of Mr. Thark?' And a frown patterned her smooth, white forehead. 'Why?'

'He's a crook,' he burst out.

Her face blanched and she braced herself against the door-frame. 'Are you sure?' she said, her voice so low that it was almost inaudible.

'I give you my word,' Nigel said solemnly.

'We can't talk on the doorstep, like this, it's absurd,' she said with a gallant smile. 'Won't you come in? No, I don't mean to meet Mr. Thark; I mean into my little study.'

He followed her into the small, pleasantly furnished room. She motioned him to a chintz-covered armchair and sat down opposite him with a little sigh. 'I can't believe that he's a crook,' she said. 'It seems impossible. Of course, I don't really *know* him, but he seems so nice. He's a sort of dealer, isn't he? He came down here to buy some things of mine, you see, and he really has been awfully kind about it. He has offered me full value for the things he wants to buy.'

'Thank God I came,' said Nigel devoutly. 'That sounds just like his little game. And do you know what he would do then? He would pay you in counterfeit notes, just as he did me.'

Judy Brown gasped with horror. 'But whatever shall I do?' she wailed. 'I need the money so badly, and he did promise to pay what I asked. Oh, surely he wouldn't cheat me! I can't believe he'd do a thing like that,' she implored. 'Here is the ring he wanted to buy, for which he offered me three hundred pounds.' She opened her clenched fist and disclosed it on her palm.

Nigel uttered a wordless exclamation. It was a lovely thing! A large cabochon emerald in an ancient silver setting, cunningly chased. For a long moment he stared at it in silence. Then he made up his mind.

'I'll buy it from you,' he said firmly, 'at the same price suggested by Thark.' That killed two birds with one stone, didn't it?

He felt pleased with himself, excited.

'No, no,' she protested, 'I couldn't possibly allow it. You have done quite enough for me already.'

'But I insist. You must look on it as a purely business proposition. I have taken a fancy to the ring, and I want to buy it. You, I happen to know, want to sell it — you said just now that you were in need of the money — and you might just as well sell it to me as to Thark.' Nigel was eager.

Judy hesitated and a warm blush spread over her face. 'You're sure you're not just doing this for — my sake?' she murmured.

'Of course not,' he assured her heartily. 'Will you sell to me? I'll write you out a cheque immediately.' He pulled out his wallet as he spoke.

The girl nodded dubiously. She seemed stunned by the unexpected turn of events.

With a firm hand, Nigel signed the cheque, and exchanged it for the ring.

'There,' he said, 'now we're both satisfied.'

'I don't know how to thank you,' said

Judy softly. 'You've been so kind.' And then, with a sudden change of tone: 'Good heavens, what am I going to say to Mr. Thark? Whatever excuse can I make?'

'Just tell him you've changed your mind and that you don't want to sell after all. He can't eat you, don't be scared.'

'Oh, dear. I suppose he can't hurt me, but it is rather awkward, isn't it? I'd better get it over at once. I'll just have to remember that he's a crook, and that'll give me courage.' She smiled. At the door she turned back. 'Oh, Mr. Armstrong, I am being a nuisance to you, but have you by any chance got a car here? You see, I would like to get this cheque banked right away — for safety — and my bank is at Bichester.'

'I'm sorry,' said Nigel regretfully, 'I'm afraid I haven't a car. I wish I had.'

'And I've missed the afternoon bus.' She bit her lower lip pensively, and a mischievous glint came into her eyes. 'Do you — do you think I could ask Mr. Thark to drive me in on his way to the station?' she dimpled.

'You might try.' Nigel grinned. 'It

would be a wholesome change for someone to get something out of *him*. Well, I wish you luck. I suppose I had better be toddling along now.'

She grasped him firmly by the hand. 'Thank you again for coming to my rescue. You've been very sweet about it all. I hope you won't regret it.'

With a swift gesture, Nigel bent and kissed her full on the lips — and was gone before she could protest.

From his cottage window, Nigel watched them set off in the cream-coloured car. He was glad he had kissed Judy, for he had an idea that he wasn't going to see her again. He tossed the ring meditatively in his hand. Funny to think of the demure little Miss Brown being in league with Oscar Thark. He had recognised the ring instantly as the one Thark had swindled from his shop. Thark must have just given it to her as a present. She must have had the dickens of a shock when he appeared out of the blue to tell her that Thark was a crook. And she was a quick thinker to have found a way out of the difficulty with such rapidity. Well, he was glad that she had thought of selling it to him as if it were her own; it was a bit of luck for him getting it back, for he had certainly never thought to see it again.

No, the country wasn't *so* dull after all — he'd enjoyed himself this afternoon. He chuckled suddenly. He would give a lot to see their faces when the bank clerk handed them back the cheque. He had prudently signed it 'N. AMESWRONG'.

I'll Wait For You

When first she saw him, Mrs. Green told herself cheerfully that he'd look a different being in a couple of months; whereas Mr. Green merely uttered a silent *My God!* In that moment, some elusive hope was shattered for them both.

God knew what *he*, the child, thought: his myopic grey eyes behind their spectacles stared out at them quite without expression. He was small for his age and not prepossessing. He was probably scared to death, poor little thing, thought Mrs. Green; what with the journey . . . and everything.

'So this is Mike,' she said. 'I hope you're going to be very happy with us, dear,' was what she began to say, and then she could have bitten her tongue off at the clumsy ineptitude. Her carefully rehearsed speech vanished from her mind. She smiled and patted his shoulder. 'This is Uncle Clive,' she said, offering him her husband instead.

His cold little hand gave Mr. Green's a limp, reluctant shake. He did not reciprocate their smiles. In fact, they could get practically no response out of him at all. On the way home, Mrs. Green pointed out to him all the things he might be supposed to be interested in: the school he would be going to, the river where some day Uncle Clive might take him fishing, the playing fields. He stared blankly each time in the direction she indicated, but made no comment. Till even Mrs. Green's loquaciousness began to flag and she fell silent.

It was bound to be awkward at first, she told herself; bound to be. It must take him a little while to settle down. It was better when they arrived at the house, because he had to be taken around and shown his room and have it all explained to him, all the rituals and ceremonies with regulated existence in their small well-managed home — the rituals and ceremonies of an ordered life: the changing of one's shoes every time one came in or went out of the house, washing one's hands before coming to table, folding one's clothes at night, stripping off the bedclothes in the morning. (But she noticed his nails were still rimmed with black when he came down to tea. She must provide him with a *nail-cleaner*, poor child.)

There were fish fingers, baked beans, peas, and chips for tea. She had thought he would enjoy that. But he hardly touched the food, and what he did fork up she could see was churning round in his mouth like a cement mixer till at last it was washed down with a swallow of tea.

'Perhaps you'd like to go out and play in the garden for a bit,' Mrs. Green suggested, sensing misery behind his taut face.

They watched him walk slowly down the concrete path to the incinerator at the end of the garden, glance at the flat fields beyond the fence, and turn away. He found nothing to interest him in such unfamiliar surroundings. He stood in the middle of Mr. Green's neat lawn with his hands in his pockets, wondering what he was expected to do out there.

They saw him from the window, abstractedly kicking the grass. Mrs. Green caught at her husband's arm as he made to rap on the pane.

'Let him be. Just for today, dear. He'll soon get used to our ways.'

Mr. Green prodded his pipe, already conscious of a sinking regret that he had ever agreed to foster this unknown child. He should not have given in to her. Women were so emotional, he thought uneasily.

'Hope it's going to work out,' he muttered.

She laughed.

'Give him a chance, poor mite! It's worse for him than for us.' She pulled him away.

But when next they looked out he was still in the same place, forlorn as a scarecrow. Mrs. Green tapped on the window and beckoned him in.

The boy seemed to settle down well enough. He was not a difficult child. He was as quiet and obedient as ever they had dared hope. And yet . . . disappointing. So unresponsive to all the treats they had devised to give him pleasure: the 'nice' neighbourhood children they had asked to tea (but they didn't seem to hit it off; the party was not a success); the books they had chosen for him, redolent with enchanted memories of their own childhoods, awakened nothing in him (it seemed he did not care for reading, except for those vulgar, illiterate comics).

Mrs. Green kept reminding herself that they must be patient. He was an odd little creature. Never smiled. And his rare laugh was more a sardonic bark than the wild cackles and explosions of mirth one expected from children. His eyes, staring palely through their glasses, were not like a child's eyes at all. They lacked altogether that touching look of innocence and trust. It struck Mr. Green they resembled rather the eyes of a soldier returning from the desolations of war.

Of course, they knew it must have been dreadful for the child. But the best thing he could do, they were both agreed, was to forget it. Because — this was the point they wanted him to understand — life wasn't like that *really*.

It was somewhat easier once school started again and his day was filled with the routine of schoolwork. At least, it was easier for Mrs. Green. The day seemed lighter when he was not there — which was something she did not confess even to Mr. Green. It was not that he was troublesome or restless: he would sit for half an hour together, his hands squeezed between his knees, staring at nothing. It wasn't natural for a child to be so quiet and still. The Greens might not have children of their own, but they knew that much.

He made no friends. Or, he did once come home accompanied by a small boy they had never seen before, and announced that he had brought Brian back to tea. But Mrs. Green wasn't having any of that. She said firmly that Brian could not come to tea without his mother's permission, and Mike must not invite people without asking her first. Brian went away, and Mike did not repeat the experiment.

There seemed to be nothing he wanted to do — a state of affairs adults find peculiarly irritating in children, feeling that the world is so full of a number of things that they all jolly well ought to be as happy as kings. Mr. Green did his best to interest him in his attempts at carpentry, in gardening, in fishing, in stamps. But nothing attracted him. Or nothing except the picture over the fireplace.

It was not the sort of picture one would expect to find in that house, and in fact it was only there because it had been painted by Mr. Green's great-grandfather, and on that account alone he was rather proud of it. There had been a fashion for such pictures in the mid-nineteenth century: romantic landscapes painted on glass — rocks, waterfalls, lakes, ruined castles, mountains, all bathed in a curiously translucent atmosphere, effected by its glass ground.

Mike was fascinated by it. He longed to know where it was and was disappointed that Uncle Clive couldn't tell him. The fact that it was painted by Uncle's great-grandfather shed a mysterious glamour over both the picture and his uncle.

'Do you think the place is still there?' he used to ask him.

'I expect so,' Mr. Green would say, not wanting to disappoint the boy by telling him that it probably depicted an ideal landscape and not a real place at all.

It was certainly real to Mike. The sort of place he'd have liked to live in. In a funny sort of way, the child did *live* there, if one can be said to *live* where one's thoughts are rather than where one's body is. It was a private retreat to him when things became unbearable. He would leave the beastly world behind and go off on a little spree in his mind, up the winding track to the deserted castle, listening to the waterfall thundering down into the lake below . . . Up there, he had the world to himself: there was no one in the castle, no one in the roughly daubed cottages with their windows crudely latticed in brown lines (as though the artist had suddenly decided to play noughts and crosses on his picture); all was freedom and tranquillity. Though he might have been there only a minute or two, it was like a little holiday for him, and when Auntie Doris called him to perform some small task, he came back with his heart eased.

The school holidays themselves, he found pretty dull. He had no friends and there was nothing to do. Only the countryside to ramble in, trees to climb, woods to explore.

But to enjoy that, one had to know how to use one's eyes, and that was something Mike had never been taught. He was a town child, and he missed the pleasures of town life: the cinemas, the amusement arcades, the gangs, the exploits in derelict tenements, the shop-pinching raids. What could the countryside offer to compare with that?

He had to admit it was pleasant to eat out of doors. Whenever it was not actually raining, Mrs. Green sent him off for the day with a bottle of fruitade plus sandwiches and chocolate biscuits. It was almost as much a relief to him as it was to her to have him out from under her feet.

On one such day, he was making his way along a narrow lane between hedgerows, kicking a stone before him for company, when he saw a girl coming towards him. She was a fattish sort of girl of thirteen or so with a pale face and lank, ragged-looking hair. He had never seen her in school, and yet she couldn't be a summer visitor because she was wearing a kind of cotton overall that looked as though it didn't belong to her.

'Hullo, fatty!' he called rudely. But she took no notice. Didn't even glance in his direction. Didn't even move in to the coarse grass edging the lane as a car whizzed round the bend behind her . . .

'*Look out!*' he shouted, as the car advanced with alarming speed. There was only just time to push her into the hedge: he felt the hot wind on his legs as the car flew past.

She scrambled upright and began to flail at him with her arms. 'Here, lay off! What you doing?' he exclaimed.

She responded with something entirely unintelligible.

'That car would have knocked you down,' he said, shaking her arm roughly and pointing to the car in the distance already no larger than a Matchbox toy. She looked from it to him, puzzled.

'Di'n't you hear it?'

The girl again uttered two strange inarticulate sounds and put one hand over her ear. Then Mike understood. She was trying to say, *I'm deaf*. Rotten luck for her, he reflected.

Then he thought proudly, *I saved her life*. For some reason, it gave him a feeling of having some proprietary right over her. Vaguely, he recalled being told that in China, if you saved a man from drowning he became your responsibility for the rest of his life. At the time it had sounded potty. For who would ever save anyone if they were going to be lumbered afterwards? But now he understood. He felt differently: he didn't want to lose her.

He waved an arm at the horizon, and said loudly and slowly: '*Where* . . . *are* . . . *you* . . . *going*?' But the girl shook her head.

She started walking again, and he had to hurry to keep up with her. Where was she from, then? he asked. He couldn't understand what she was saying, and when she saw his face screwed up with an intensity of concentration, she halted and, watching him closely, repeated the grunted syllables over and over as clearly as she could.

'Oh, *Chankerdown*!' he said at last. 'The loony-bin!' He hesitated, looked away, and then blurted out: 'You're not a loony, are you?'

Vehemently she shook her head. 'Hey *hink* I ang,' she said.

They thought she was loony, of course, because she was deaf and couldn't speak properly. So she'd been put with the loonies. 'You're running away then?' the boy inquired. His heart glowed within him. It even darted through his mind that he could run away too, and he wondered that it had never occurred to him before. Except that he had nowhere to go. But then neither had she. She needed someone to help her, he thought. For one, that overall-thing was probably a sort of uniform which anyone might recognize.

In a hazel copse not far away, they sat

down comfortably, and shared his sandwiches and bottle of cola. He learned that her name was Lizzie and that she had been sent to Chankerdown two years ago when she was eleven, on the pretext that her mother couldn't manage her. Couldn't be bothered with her, more like. She made beds, washed up, and polished the corridors from early morning till bedtime. It was not the work she minded, but being trapped in a way of life she could see no end to. How was she ever to get out of that place? It frightened her to think of spending the rest of her life there. It frightened Mike to find that she could not read or write or count. He could not think what would become of her in the open world. She was worse off than he was, even more hopelessly at sea.

Something was released in him at this perception, something like a small stone in his chest, as heavy as a load of brick. He had found someone at last who he could talk to.

Kneeling there among the dry dead leaves, swirling his hands in them as he spoke, he poured out all the pent-up horror of the past and the misery of the present. The stone-deaf girl kept her eyes attentively on his frantic little white face all the while, as though she could hear and understand what he was saying.

He described, exactly as if he was watching it happen before his eyes, how he had seen his dad kill his mum; described the dishevelled bed and his mum crouched up against the head with her knees pressed to her chin to protect herself; and the wild cry she gave as his dad caught her wrist and pulled her free and the blood leaped out across the dirty sheets; and it had all happened so quickly that he hadn't even had the time to spring out of his bed to try and save her; and then he was too frightened to go to her in case his dad did him in too . . . And then . . . and then . . . and then they took his dad away, and he was taken off somewhere else, and after that it was all a muddle of being in one place after another and people asking him questions and there being no one ever again who belonged to him. And now he was with these people who called themselves his uncle and auntie, only they weren't, and it was just a place where people had put him because they didn't know what to do with him, just like they'd put her in Chankerdown to get rid of her.

The violent tangle of words slowed down and ceased. An awkward silence fell. He had spoken of things he had kept locked inside him for a long time. The girl understood only that he was distressed. She leaned forward suddenly and shyly kissed his cheek. He pulled back, red-faced, and then with a gulp flung himself on to her breast, sobs bursting painfully from him. She put her arms round him.

'We gotter be careful,' he impressed upon her. 'By now they may be looking for you. You better come back with me. I'll look after you. Understand? You come with me.' He pointed to her and to himself. It was really quite easy to make her understand; she wasn't a bit stupid.

Mike had a plan. His idea was to smuggle her into the house before the Greens got back from their weekly shopping expedition to the market town, and hide her in his room. The next day, while Mrs. Green was out (she'd be bound to go out sometime), he'd take one of her dresses for Liz to wear, collect what money he could find and Liz could carry a shopping bag with bread and tinned meat and stuff in it: they'd live like tramps, sleeping in barns and doing odd jobs when they needed food or money. He explained his plans to her enthusiastically, his grey eyes sparkling with excitement.

The house was empty. In the kitchen he cut them some thick buttery slices of bread and jam, and then, taking her hand, he took her round the house pointing out to her all the things he liked and all the things he hated. He showed her the glass picture.

'That's where I'd like to live; no school, no grown-ups, no one to *interfere*. We'd go fishing on the lake in that boat. I bet there'd be a lot of fish in a lake like that. And I could catch a rabbit or two. We'd be all right, wouldn't we?'

'Eee ee aw igh,' Lizzie agreed with a broad grin.

They smiled at each other, rapt in their childish dream.

'Well, it must be somewhere, that place. People don't paint pictures of places that don't exist, do they? We've only got to find it, Liz.'

He caught sight of Aunt Doris coming up the path with her arms full of packages, and bundled Lizzie up the stairs into his room. He put his fingers to his lips, and pushed her quickly into the wardrobe, gesturing to her to stay there and not make a sound. He shut her in and picked up a hairbrush as Mrs. Green came running upstairs to put her outdoor things away.

After tea, Mr. Green wanted help to stake the dahlias in the front garden, and it was half past nine before Mike could get away. His little room was full of dusk, but he did not turn on the light. Outside, the sky was a dim translucent blue, like the sky in his picture, holding the last reflected light from the departed sun. The girl was so cramped that he had to help her out of the wardrobe or she would have fallen. He gestured towards the bed.

Lizzie looked the other way while he undressed. She unfastened her overall and hung it inside the wardrobe, and in her vest and knickers scrambled in against the wall. Mike climbed in beside her. They lay down straight and mute as corpses.

Tomorrow, everything was going to be wonderful, he thought. Even today had been the happiest day he'd had since —

He raised himself up on his elbow and bumped his nose against her face in a sort of kiss: 'Goodnight, Lizzie. I do like you,' he said, and slid down again with his back to her, very red in the face.

He lay quietly for a long time, memorizing all he would have to do next day. He would pretend she was his sister, and their parents were dead, and they were going to live with their grandmother. Their grandmother lived in — Cornwall — yes, that was a good long way away . . . in a town called . . . he must remember the name of a Cornish town . . . St. Ives, that would do — 'As I was going to St. Ives, I met a man with seven wives'. He was getting very sleepy, but he

274

had to keep awake till they'd gone to bed. What was his grandmother's name? Mrs. Laburnham, he thought drowsily, and she lives at Cherry Tree Cottage.

It was so relaxing to have these problems solved that he nearly fell asleep. He might even have done so for a short while, but the quiet footsteps on the stairs roused him. He pushed Lizzie flat and pulled the clothes up to cover her head.

The door opened. He heard Mrs. Green tiptoe across the room to draw the curtains together — he'd forgotten to pull them. She came and stood by his bed, looking down at him. He held his breath.

'Are you awake, dear?' she said softly.

He gave a long sigh. 'Yes, Auntie,' he muttered sleepily.

'You've got your glasses on still.' Gently, she drew them off and placed them on the table beside him, then bent to give him her customary goodnight kiss. She leaned a hand on the far side of his body to support herself. The kiss never reached him. She straightened herself abruptly. 'What on earth have you got in the bed with you?'

'Nothing, Auntie.' His heart began to thump like a soldier's drum.

Mrs. Green whipped off the bed-clothes, exposing the boy in his pyjamas and Lizzie, her mouth open and her face flushed with sleep, in her grubby vest and knickers. Mrs. Green stared at them as though they were naked. She went crimson as a radish.

'You filthy little beast! You filthy little beast! At your age!' she stammered. 'How dare you? In my house, after all I've done for you! Get her up out of there, *this instant.*'

He had to shake her to make her wake. As soon as she saw his frightened face, Lizzie understood that something terrible had happened and it was all up with them. She sat up beside him, clutching his damp, bony little hand, and gazing in fright at the angry strange woman. The look of her was enough to set Lizzie scrambling awkwardly off the bed.

'Tell her to put her clothes on,' Mrs. Green said, not even looking in her direction. But Lizzie was already humbly climbing into her cotton slip and overall, fastening the buttons with trembling fingers. She didn't need to hear what the woman was saying to know that the air was full of hatred and contempt.

'Who is this girl and where is she from?' Mrs. Green demanded.

Mike ran his tongue across his lips.

'She's my sister.'

'You haven't got a sister.'

'I have! I have!'

'What's up?' interpolated Mr. Green, sticking his head round the door on his way back from the bathroom.

'He's been carrying on with this girl.'

'I wasn't,' Mike protested. 'I never done nothing.'

'I found them in bed together. He wants a good whipping.'

'Well, well, we'll see. She's only a child herself, dear.'

'That's what makes it so disgusting. Get her out of here. It makes me sick to see her.'

'You can't turn her out at this time of night. Where's she from?'

Inevitably, it was revealed that the girl was from the mental hospital on the hill.

'But she's not a loony,' Mike insisted. 'It's only that she's deaf and can't talk proper, so they put her there to get her out of the way. Don't make her go back there, Uncle Clive.'

'She's run away, is that it?'

The Greens were not on the phone, but the hospital was only ten minutes away by car. Obviously she had to go back there, said Mr. Green; the hospital authorities were responsible for her, had probably already informed the police that she was missing.

Mike did his best to explain to Uncle Clive why she should not be sent back, but he hadn't the words to make him understand. As Mr. Green pushed the girl ahead of him, Mike clung to his arm and kicked him and began to scream . . . But Lizzie didn't struggle at all. She followed Mr. Green meekly down the path, climbed into the car, and was driven away without once looking round. With tears streaming down his face, Mike watched the car disappear.

For the next few days, he went about as grey and silent as a little ghost. It had been a great shock to him: not only the shattering of his rainbow-bright dream, but encountering Mr. and Mrs. Green with their kind masks off.

And then he vanished. At least, he was late for tea and wasn't even back at bedtime. It occurred to them that he must have had an accident. At half past ten, Mr. Green went to the police and said their foster-child had gone missing, and he and his wife were afraid he might have been knocked down by a car.

Because the boy had taken nothing with him, not a single article of clothing nor even any of his small worthless treasures, it did not enter their minds that he might have run away. But the police did not ignore the possibility. As the days passed and the boy was not found, they began to ask questions.

Was he unhappy? Had he been in difficulties at school? Had the Greens punished him recently? Had they had occasion to hit him? Was any money missing? Had he any savings he might have taken with him? Where did the Greens think he would be most likely to have gone if he had run away?

But all these questions the Greens could only answer in the negative. They simply did not know, had no idea. Their innocent ignorance contributed to their feeling of guilt. They did not see how they were to blame, but they felt that people — the police, the neighbours — *thought* they were.

People began to say he must have been murdered by one of these hopeless sex-maniacs, and at the weekend everyone joined in the search of woods and ditches and river. But no trace of him was found, not so much as a discarded shoe.

But mention of a sex-maniac reminded Mr. Green of the girl from Chankerdown, and on sheer speculation he went up there. It was then they found the first and only clue in the whole case. A postcard with a picture of some cats in a cat-hairdresser's on one side, addressed on the reverse in a childish hand to *Deaf and Dumb Lizzie, Chankerdown Hospital*, with the simple message: *I'LL WAIT FOR YOU*.

The police supposed it meant he was hanging around in the locality waiting for her to escape again, but they never came across him. Then — or ever.

When the boy had been gone so long that it became apparent even to the most hopeful that he was not likely to be found alive, Mr. Green had a most unpleasant experience. A hallucination, no doubt. Or the effects of a disordered stomach. Or a trick of the moonlight. For it happened when he was alone one evening, Mrs. Green having gone to bed with a headache.

He was brooding in the dusky room, sucking his empty pipe and staring blankly at the glass picture — partly because one must rest one's eyes somewhere, and partly because the moonlight was on that patch of wall.

Something — a mark, a movement, a shadow on the picture — caught his attention. He sat up, leaned forward, staring. There had been, he was *absolutely certain*, two little white sailing boats like seagulls poised motionless in the middle of the lake. Now there was only one. The other was at the far side of the lake, plainly visible against the woolly brown of the distant trees.

He thought he must be going mad. He turned away, blinking, and when he looked again, the little boat had traversed a third of the lake. He watched it, fascinated and incredulous, advancing towards the clump of reeds in the foreground. *I'm asleep, of course*, he thought, for he felt numb and heavy as one does in a nightmare. He wanted to get up and turn on the light, but he could not move.

The boat slid into the reeds, and he saw the helmsman climbing out and making fast. It was only a tiny figure, naturally (the boat itself was not larger, now that it was in the foreground, than Mr. Green's thumbnail), but he recognized it with horror: the familiar shape of a small, pale-faced, drab-haired boy in glasses, wearing the clothes he had been wearing the day he disappeared.

The boy turned, appeared to look straight at Mr. Green, and came (Mr. Green could not tell how, but in a moment he had traversed the inch or two of painting representing a hundred yards of actual space) and pressed his face against the glass as though it were a window-pane. The grubby little hands leaned on the glass on either side. The nose was squashed into a greenish triangle, Mr. Green observed. The pale eyes behind their spectacles *gazed* straight into Mr. Green's with an unfathomable expression. The mouth was open wide. But whether it was calling for help, or jeering, or even laughing, Mr. Green could not tell.

But the question that rattled in Mr. Green's skull was: How could the child be *in* the picture? How could a three-dimensional being exist in a two-dimensional world? The notion overwhelmed him. He stumbled to his feet and ran out of the room. He reached the bathroom just in time. 'I mustn't speak of this to Doris,' he thought as he vomited up his terror. 'She must never know.'

At that moment, Mrs. Green appeared in the doorway. 'Clive dear, what's the matter?'

'It's all right, I'll be better in a minute. You go back to bed, dear. Sardines always have upset me.'

We do hope that you have enjoyed reading this large print book.

Did you know that all of our titles are available for purchase?

We publish a wide range of high quality large print books including:
Romances, Mysteries, Classics
General Fiction
Non Fiction and Westerns

Special interest titles available in large print are:
The Little Oxford Dictionary
Music Book, Song Book
Hymn Book, Service Book

Also available from us courtesy of Oxford University Press:
Young Readers' Dictionary
(large print edition)
Young Readers' Thesaurus
(large print edition)

For further information or a free brochure, please contact us at:
Ulverscroft Large Print Books Ltd.,
The Green, Bradgate Road, Anstey,
Leicester, LE7 7FU, England.
Tel: (00 44) **0116 236 4325**
Fax: (00 44) **0116 234 0205**

STING OF DEATH

Shelley Smith

Devoted wife and mother Linda Campion is found dead in her hall, sprawled on the marble floor, clutching a Catholic medallion of Saint Thérèse. An accidental tumble over the banisters? A suicidal plummet? Or is there an even more sinister explanation? As the police investigation begins to unearth family secrets, it becomes clear that all was not well in the household: Linda's husband Edmund — not long home from the war — has disappeared; and one of their guests has recently killed himself . . .

MRS. WATSON AND THE SHAKESPEARE CURSE

Michael Mallory

London, 1906. One of the world's foremost Shakespeare scholars presents a paper at Madame Tussaud's which claims that the real author of the works accredited to the Bard of Avon was none other than Queen Elizabeth I. Few in his audience, including the redoubtable Amelia Watson, wife of Doctor John H., take him seriously — but shortly afterward he is found murdered in his hotel room. Worse — Amelia's actor friend, Harry Benbow, is falsely accused of the crime. Can Amelia clear his name before Scotland Yard catch up to him?

SCREAMWORLD

Edmund Glasby

When the insurance official sent to check out an accident at a gruesome theme park called Screamworld goes missing, private investigator John Brent is called in. Could the disappearance be linked with the unusual creator of the park — or are there other forces at work? What Brent finds behind the park's ghastly façade far exceeds his worst expectations, and threatens to drag him into a terrifying maelstrom of murder and madness, as the true purpose of the main attraction becomes all too clear . . .